# SUNDANCE:
# THE WILD STALLIONS

Luke Drury was one of the toughest men in the West. He wanted the Nez Perce stallions, and would steal them if necessary. Only Sundance, personal friend of Wild Bill Hickok and Calamity Jane, and the English woman stood between Drury and what could amount to the fall of the whole Nez Perce nation.

# JOHN BENTEEN

---

# SUNDANCE: THE WILD STALLIONS

## Complete and Unabridged

# LINFORD
*Leicester*

First published in the
United States of America


First Linford Edition
published July 1992

British Library CIP Data

Benteen, John
   Sundance: the wild stallions.—Large print ed.—
Linford western library
I. Title II. Series
823.914 [F]

ISBN 0-7089-7181-4


Published by
F. A. Thorpe (Publishing) Ltd.
Anstey, Leicestershire

Set by Words & Graphics Ltd.
Anstey, Leicestershire
Printed and bound in Great Britain by
T. J. Press (Padstow) Ltd., Padstow, Cornwall

# 1

HE came into Deadwood from the west, a big man on a tall Appaloosa stallion, horse and rider alike marked by hard traveling. Because he knew that he was one of the most hated and most feared men on this side of the Mississippi, and, likely, in certain places on the other side of it as well — Chicago, Washington, New York — Sundance rode with caution, his eyes missing nothing as he came down the gulch that almost swallowed the booming town, his left hand on the stallion's reins and his right never very far from the butt of the Colt on his thigh. He was not an outlaw, there was no price, officially, that he knew of, on his head, but he knew that now, in the summer of 1878, a great many people wanted him dead. Some were red, most were white; he could never

1

tell when they would make a try at him. He could have hidden, he could have traveled with the stealth of a wolf, but that was not his way. He was not ashamed of anything he had done, and he rode proudly wherever he went, his whole bearing a challenge. He was, after all, a fighting man by trade, and anybody who took him on had better be prepared to pay the price.

A letter had brought him to Deadwood, one too important to ignore, but he hated the sight of the ugly, swarming town. Not much over five years before, the Black Hills of Dakota had been the sacred lands of the Sioux Nation, their revered *Paha Sapa*. Then Custer had found gold here and had broadcast his finding to the world to build his own reputation, and the whites had swarmed in irresistibly. Now Custer was dead at Little Big Horn, but that was scant consolation. The Sioux, and their allies, the Cheyennes, were broken. Crazy Horse was dead, Dull Knife had surrendered, Sitting Bull was five hundred miles deep in Canada with a remnant of the Hunkpapa, and white men scurried over the Black Hills like ants over the carcass of some magnificent dead animal. Sundance, who was half Cheyenne and half white, with a foot in both the worlds and never wholly at home in either, was revolted by the scars of mining and logging on what had once been a fine wilderness, with great riches for those who knew properly how to harvest them. The Sioux had harvested those riches for hundreds of years and had never changed the land; the whites had been here for four years and already had nearly ruined it.

Eyes turned to follow him as the stallion's hoofs made sucking noises in the deep mud of Main Street. His big shoulders bulked beneath a buckskin shirt worked with beads and porcupine quills in the Northern Cheyenne way, richly fringed. Narrow hips and long legs were encased in denim pants; his feet in Cheyenne moccasins. The .45

Colt and the Winchester carbine in the saddle scabbard were of the latest models. But what really drew startled gazes was his face.

It was a Cheyenne's countenance, with prominent cheekbones, great nose like an eagle's beak, wide mouth, strong chin, and skin the color of weathered copper. But, in startling contrast, the hair that spilled from beneath his battered sombrero to the collar of the buckskin shirt was a silky yellow the color of fresh-minted gold, and his eyes were a cold rain-cloud colored blue-gray. Most half breeds had black eyes, some had red hair; Sundance was a one in ten-thousand genetic mixture, and the effect was striking. It generated cautious appraisal in the eyes of the white men on the plank sidewalks, and something else in the eyes of the white women, who were mostly whores of varying status and price. It would be a while yet before decent women came to Deadwood in any number. Those that were here now knew a man when they saw one.

Scarred, timber-clad hills loomed on either side, and the town clung to their flanks almost desperately. The mud was better than two feet deep in the street, for water sluiced down into the gulch as if it were a gutter, and there was always plenty of rain in the Black Hills, even when the rest of Dakota parched. The mud didn't seem to dismay anybody; it took strong oxen and big mules to haul freight up and down the steep grades through the muck, and teamsters cursed and cracked their whips, riding or slogging alongside, their outfits jamming the narrow way. There were horsemen, too, and miners on foot, crossing at points where timbers had been thrown down in the mud, spouting colorful profanity when they bogged down. There were, as well, all the scavengers who came to prey on any goldstrike: gamblers, prostitutes, gunmen; and mingled with them were a great many Chinese, in baggy clothes, their saffron skins and dangling pigtails setting them apart. Sundance had never seen so many in any other Western town this side of San Francisco. Brought in to build railroads as cheap labor, they had flocked to Dakota at the news of gold. Surveying the crowd as the Appaloosa stallion, Eagle, moved along, Sundance never forgot for a moment that this was where his old friend Hickok had died two years before, shot from behind. If he had needed any warning, that would have been enough . . . Then, suddenly, in the very heart of town, he drew rein, hard. If he had not, the stallion would have walked right over the man.

It was a Chinese, baggy pants tucked into big rubber boots. He had left the sidewalk, started across the street through the muck, bogged down, tripped, fallen. Covered with mud, he got to his feet again and tried to pull a boot loose from the sucking swamp that passed for a street. If he had been of normal size, he would have had less trouble, but, elderly — Sundance guessed at least sixty — and wraith-slim and not much taller than a twelve-year-old American child, he was mired fast. Sundance was about to turn Eagle toward him and offer him a stirrup for leverage when he saw the bull team.

It was a hitch of four oxen coming up the street, pulling a high-sided freight wagon loaded with lumber. Beside it slogged a giant of a man, not tall, but enormously broad, a blackbearded teamster in red shirt, canvas pants, and jackboots rising above his knees. He was wielding a nine-foot drover's whip on his oxen, flicking bits of fur and skin with every snap. The bogged-down Chinaman was directly in his path.

When the teamster saw him, he spouted deep-voiced profanity. "Git th' livin' hell outa the way, you yella bastard!" he finished, and his whip flicked out and made a sound like a pistol shot. The old Chinese stared at him, tried desperately to move, and fell down again.

The teamster, seeing that, laughed, showing greenish teeth in the depths of his beard. "Awright, damn your yellow hide! You won't move, I'll walk right over your Chink carcass! Yahh, Buck!" The whip spurred the lead oxen into faster motion. The wagon creaked and rumbled, and it was not ten feet from the helplessly trapped old man, who, once again on his feet, fought desperately to get loose from the mud.

Sundance's mouth thinned.

There was no doubt about it. The teamster intended to drive his oxen directly over the old man, let their splayed hoofs bear him down, let the wheels of the heavy wagon grind him into the mud. Sundance saw the glitter in the teamster's eyes, his wide, expectant grin. He saw, too, the panic on the withered, lined face of the old Chinese. Another minute and doom would be upon the man.

Sundance touched Eagle with his heels.

The big stallion plunged forward through the mud. Sundance turned him, planted the stud's curiously spotted body like a wall between the advancing oxen and the bogged old man. Instinctively confronted by that barrier, the team halted.

The teamster's face twisted. "Hey, there, you, you goddam Injun! Git the hell outa my road!"

"In a minute," Sundance said. Then, to the Chinese: "Take my stirrup."

"Savvee," the man gasped, and Sundance felt his weight against the leather.

The teamster stared, the lash of his whip lying extended on the muddy surface of the street. "Well, hell's fahr," he said, and the lash, as he flicked his wrist, coiled back, struck forward like an angry snake.

Eagle, the stallion, grunted as its tip chopped skin and flesh from his rump, but, at pressure on the reins, he stood

9

fast, blocking the oxen.

There had been no apparent motion, but now Sundance's Colt was in his hand, lined on the second button of the bullwhacker's shirt, and the half-breed's face was like a mask of hammered copper. The teamster, looking up at it, knew he was as close to death as he would ever come until his judgement day; and he froze.

The Chinese was on his feet now, leaning against Eagle's flank. The incident had caught the attention of people on the sidewalks, and they were watching. Sundance said, earing back the hammer of the gun, "You. Bring me that bullwhip." His voice was very quiet.

"I — "

"Bring it here. And if you try to use it again, I'll not kill you. I'll just cripple you for life."

The man looked up at Sundance, and what he saw in those raincloud eyes leached the color from beneath his skin. He hesitated for one second

10

more, then slogged forward.

"Pass it up butt first," Sundance said.

He looked down into a flat, vicious, stupid face. The face of a man who thought that his color gave him the right of life or death over everyone else whose skin was of any darker or different hue. Sundance felt a bitter, searing surge of hatred. Custer had been like that, handsome and well-educated as he was. He fought back the impulse to pull the trigger of the Colt. Anyhow, he knew a way to hurt the man much worse.

He took the whip. "Turn around," he said.

"Why — "

"I said turn around." Sundance jerked the muzzle of the Colt.

For a second longer, the teamster stared, then he turned.

"Bend over," said Sundance, transferring the revolver to his left hand, taking the whipstock in his right. He let the black, braided, nine-foot lash trail out on the mud. "Stand, Eagle," he murmured, and the horse was like a rock beneath him. The teamster stood motionless. "Damn you," Sundance grated, "I said, bend over!"

"I — Damn it, no!"

Sundance fired the gun. It's report was thunderous; the slug ripped between the teamster's legs, dangerously close to the crotch, splatted into mud. *I said, bend over!*" Sundance roared.

The teamster looked into his eyes and slowly turned. Then he bent.

"Farther!" Sundance snapped.

Reluctantly, the bullwhacker hunkered lower, beefy buttocks bulging his canvas pants as he presented his rump to Sundance. Sundance grinned coldly; his right hand moved. He had learned long ago to make a drover's whip sing; and the long, black lash was like a living thing as it slashed back, then forward.

The teamster howled as its tip chopped fabric from his pants, meat from his right buttock. He jerked erect.

Sundance yelled, "Down!"

Face working, the man looked over his shoulder into the muzzle of the Colt. Then he bent again and once more the whip came forward, and he yelled as it chopped his other buttock. Little stains of red appeared on opposite sides of the seat of his pants, and it would be a week, Sundance thought with grim satisfaction, before he sat down comfortably again.

Onlookers ranged on the sidewalks jeered and shouted with laughter. The teamster made a blubbering noise.

"All right," Sundance said. "Straighten up and turn around."

When the man obeyed, face pale, hands tenderly touching his rump, Sundance holstered the gun and with a swift motion drew the footlong Bowie that rode in a beaded sheath behind it on his hip. The blade, razor-sharp, flashed, and the severed lash of the whip fell into the mud like the body of a snake. Sundance tossed the handle after it.

"Next time," he said harshly, "you think before you try to run down a man, any man. And you think even harder before you use one of those on a man's horse. Now, listen to me. You stay clear of me while I'm in Deadwood. You bother me again, I'll most likely kill you."

He meant it and the teamster understood that. Face pale, he turned wordlessly away. Sundance lifted Eagle's reins and the Appaloosa walked across the street, the Chinese still holding to the stirrup. Plastered with mud from head to foot, he gained the sidewalk, and Sundance looked down into a seamed, withered yellow face stringy with long gray wisps of mustache and chinwhiskers. The man began to speak rapidly in Chinese. Sundance shrugged. "No savvee. But it's alright. Only, next time be more careful." He turned the stallion and rode away, leaving the man there on the walk. Across the way, people still laughed at the teamster, who shouted profanely at his oxen and lashed them with the end of his severed whip. Sundance's mouth thinned. It had not been smart to draw more attention to himself in such a way, but the teamster represented a breed of man he hated, a kind of white all too common out here. Anyone in their estimation with a different colored skin was less than human. To him, crunching the Chinaman beneath his wagon wheels would have been no more significant than running over a stray dog. The hell of it was, Sundance thought, that in a mining camp like this, he would have taken no more punishment for it, either, than if the old man had been an animal. For that matter, he could have killed an Indian — or a half breed — in the same way, with no more penalty. *The only good Indian's a dead Indian.* That applied to half bloods, too.

Sundance spat into the mud. He had meant to go straight to the hotel to find Bucknell, but now he wanted a drink. There were plenty of saloons in

Deadwood, and it was just a matter of turning the stallion to the nearest hitchrack.

There he swung down and checked the whip-wound on the big horse's rump. It was minor, for the whip had been deflected by one of the two big buffalo-hide *parfleches*, panniers of strange shape, slung behind the cantle. The stallion, trained for running buffalo and for war, had taken far worse in its time. Sundance patted the thick neck, then went into the saloon, Carl Mann's Number Ten. He had not been here in 1876, but vaguely he remembered hearing that this was where his old friend Hickok had got it in the back of the head from Jack McCall. That was something Sundance could not understand; he himself always sat with his back to the wall in such a place. Hickok must have grown careless as he got older.

In the saloon, which was large, of rough lumber, with mounted game heads and Indian trappings — shields and bows and spears, hunting trophies of a different sort — on the wall, Sundance first surveyed the crowd, making sure that no one here was a known enemy. Even this early, there were plenty of customers, but he saw no one he knew, except for a withered crone of a woman in buckskin shirt, sombrero, black skirt, high boots, and with a gun belted around her waist. She hunched over a schooner of beer at a table in a corner, and did not look up, and Sundance let her be. He had no desire to listen to Calamity Jane Canary's drunken rantings.

Satisfied, he went to the bar and ordered two shots of whiskey. He drank the first at a gulp and carried the second with him to a table where the logs of the saloon would shield his back. There he sipped it, barely moistening his lips. Two drinks at a time was his limit. Something in him, his heritage from his Cheyenne mother, could not tolerate much alcohol. The third drink would make him roaring drunk, the fourth would turn him into a mindless, fighting animal, so, always, he was careful.

While he toyed with the glass, he thought about the errand that had brought him here. There would be no profit in it for him, but that was all right. He had just wound up a gun job in California, and even after sending most of the proceeds off to Washington, he still had a thousand dollars, which would hold him for a while. The important thing was that, if everything fell right, he might make as much as thirty or forty thousand dollars for the Nez Perces under Chief Joseph down in Kansas, crammed on to the Quapaw reserve with the Modocs, under the guns of Fort Leavenworth; and never had an Indian tribe needed that kind of money more. For them it meant the difference between life and death . . . Well, by God, he thought, he would squeeze the last, top dollar out of Bucknell. The man was rich, he could well afford to pay. After all, for him this was just a kind of amusement; for Joseph and the Nez Perce, it meant survival.

He was halfway through the second drink when a sixth sense made him lift his head. Or, possibly, it was the sound of the saloon doors closing. Anyhow, he knew at once that he was the one sought by the man who stood there just inside the room.

Then he was spotted and the man came forward, and as he did so, Sundance eased his Colt around higher on his thigh and sat up straight. During the half minute it took the man to reach him, Sundance had plenty of time to look him over, and he did not particularly like what he saw. Then the man was towering over him. "You're Sundance," he said, his voice deep.

"Yeah," said Sundance.

"My name's Drury, Luke Drury. From Oregon. Maybe you've heard of me."

Sundance's eyes ranged over Drury.

He was even taller than Sundance, about the same age, late thirties or early forties. He wore a weatherbeaten black sombrero, and beneath it his face was leathery, tanned by sun and wind, lined and seamed. His eyes were gray, his nose big, his mouth wide, chin craggy. That face told Sundance immediately that he was as tough as an old boot. The big body and the way Drury wore his two guns bore it out. Drury's shoulders were enormous, his chest thick beneath a flannel shirt and leather vest, his hips narrow, his legs long and bowed, horseman's legs. His Colts were on two separate, crisscrossed belts, their holsters tied down. Sundance felt force, power, and self-confidence radiating from the man.

"Heard of you? Sorry."

Drury grinned. "Well, now you have." He turned, let out a bellow. "Frank, bring a bottle and another glass, and not rotgut, good whiskey!"

"Yes, sir, Mr. Drury!" the bartender called.

"You don't mind if I sit down." A statement.

"Help yourself," Sundance said.

Drury hooked out a chair, dropped into it, took two black cheroots from a pocket of his vest, passed one to Sundance. Sundance accepted it, bit off the end, lit it, found it strong, but excellent. "Good cigar," he said.

"Nothing but the best for Luke Drury." Smoke drifted from the nostrils of the craggy, broken nose.

"I've been waiting for you," he added.

Sundance tensed. Nobody but Bucknell was supposed to know that he was coming to Deadwood. "Have you now?"

"That's right," Drury said. "Sundance, I'm in the horse business in a big way. I supply remounts to the Army. Sell horses to the stagecoach people, too, all up and down the west coast. I deal in nothing but the best . . ."

He paused. The bartender brought the bottle and a glass, opened the

21

bottle and poured a shot for Drury. When he left, Drury, looking straight into Sundance's eyes, went on.

"That's why I've spent a lot of time here in Deadwood, waiting for you to show up. Sundance, I want to buy the Nez Perce stallions."

Jim Sundance drained his second drink and said, "Why, Drury, I don't know what you're talking about."

Drury's face did not change, but his eyes did, becoming as hard as flakes of granite.

"Don't hand me that, Jim Sundance. You were with the Nez Perce last year during their war. You saved their horses, their very best studs and mares, and you've got 'em hid out somewhere. Six stallions and twenty-five prime mares, Appaloosas all. There ain't no better horses in the world, and I've got to have 'em. So don't look innocent. I'm offering you twenty thousand dollars for the Nez Perce stud. And by stud, I don't mean a single stallion. I mean the whole breeding bunch. So now, suppose we cut the games and get down to business. I'll give you five thousand now and fifteen thousand more when you deliver the horses to me at The Dalles. Right?"

"No," Jim Sundance said quietly. "Wrong, Drury. Very wrong."

23

## 2

FOR a second or two, Drury's face did not change. Then, to Sundance's surprise, he smiled.

"They told me you'd be hard to deal with."

"Who told you?"

"The Army."

"Why," Jim Sundance said, "the Army's given you bad information, Drury. I'm not hard to deal with. It's just that there aren't any Nez Perce horses."

Drury rolled his cheroot across his mouth, then sat up straight. "Sundance, I said, cut the games. I know all about you and I know all about those horses." He leaned forward.

"Jim Sundance," he said. "For God's sake, you're famous all across the West. Your daddy came out here from England years ago, a remittance man.

He took up trapping and trading and married a Northern Cheyenne woman. He gave you a white man's education, but you grew up among the Injuns, not just the Cheyennes, all the Injuns. Nick Sundance, as he called himself, traded with the tribes all the way from Canada to Mexico and you learned all their languages and customs, got yourself adopted into most of 'em. You're a Cheyenne Dog Soldier in good standin', but you can quote Shakespeare or the Bible if you got to, or rattle off Apache or Yaqui just as easy as Cheyenne or Sioux."

"That's a big rep you're giving me," Sundance said quietly.

"They say you've earned it. I've heard the story about the six scalps . . . "

"Have you now?"

"It was in the early '60's, and you were shy of twenty at the time. Your old man and your mama went into Bent's Fort to trade and you rode along. The tribes were in, and there was a fiesta and horse racin' and you

25

stayed behind for the fun when your folks struck out north again. When you caught up with 'em, you found 'em dead. Somebody'd robbed and killed 'em and on top of that, before they killed your mama — ''

"That's enough," Sundance said in an iron voice.

"So . . . " Drury nodded. "Three Pawnees and three drunk whites, and they split up to throw you off their trails. But you followed those trails, all six separate ones, until you ran 'em down to their end. It took you over a year, but — They say you got a war shield, like any other Injun. And there's six scalps on it, three black and the others different colors — and none of the men they come from died easy."

Sundance leaned back. "Who told you all this?"

"Phil Sheridan. Commander of all the troops in the West. He knows you well. Even, he said, used to like you."

Sundance let his eyes narrow. After all, it was Sheridan who had made that statement about good Indians and dead ones . . . "Go on," he said. "What else do you know?"

"You were, the way I heard it, kind of crazy after that. You had a big mad still to work out, and you drifted east, got sucked up in the war along the Kansas-Missouri border. Rode with the bushwhackers there, didn't really care which side you fought on. But you came out of that mess a prime hand with a pistol. You were already good with Indian weapons, that made you a first class *pistolero*."

"Sheridan told you a lot," Sundance said thinly.

"A lot of it just floats around, and a man picks it up." Drury poured another drink. "You came back west with a crazy idea in mind . . . "

"It didn't seem so crazy," Sundance said unvoluntarily.

"It seems pretty crazy now. You figured there was room enough for the whites and Injuns to live together out here. Thought that since you were both, you could help 'em work together. You even scouted for the Army for a while ... "

Sundance said, "I don't have to explain anything to you, Drury. But since you seem to get around a lot and talk a lot, maybe I'd better give you the straight of it. Yeah, I thought the Indians and whites could learn to live together. A lot of both races thought the same. I went by the treaties, at first. If the Indians broke the treaties, I helped the Army against 'em — " He turned his empty glass in a circle. "It didn't take me long to find out it wasn't the Army that needed help. It didn't take me long to find out that the whites broke two treaties for every one the Indians violated — " His mouth twisted. "No matter what they said, all they wanted was everything the tribes had. I got wise after a while."

"You sure as hell did. You've been fightin' on the Indian side for years. They say you realized a long time ago the real war was in Washington

28

and even hired a high-priced lobbyist to work for the Indians in Congress. They say you pay him by hirin' out your guns. I've heard something else, too. That you were at Little Big Horn when Custer got rubbed out. Not with the Army, but with the Injuns. There's even rumors that it was you yourself that shot Custer. You'd had a runnin' fight with him for years."

Sundance's face froze and he said nothing. But, of course, it was true. Except for Sitting Bull and a remnant of the Hunkpapa Sioux living in Canada, most of the Indians who were at Little Big Horn had come in, and, naturally, the word had spread . . .

"Anyhow," Drury continued, "you've been mixed up in most every major Injun fight in the past ten years, one side or the other. And you were mixed up with the Nez Perces, too."

He held out the bottle. "Have a drink, Sundance."

Sundance looked at it, was tempted, shook his head. "No, thanks."

Drury poured another one, tossed it off, leaned back in his chair, and an easy grin spread across his face. "Truth to tell, Sundance, I don't blame you and I don't really give a damn about the right and wrong of it. God knows, if I'd been Injun, or even part Injun, likely I'd have been right there with you. There are a lot of people out here who don't approve of what happened to the Nez Perce. But that's water over the dam right now. What matters is the Nez Perce horses."

He leaned forward.

"Sundance, they say the Nez Perce are the smartest Injuns in the country. Up there on the Idaho-Washington line, they've been breedin' horses in a way all their own — those big, strong mountain horses with the spots like somebody had throwed a bucket of paint all over 'em — the Appaloosas."

He drained his glass. "The Appaloosas! They can run all day and night over country that'd break an ordinary cavalry mount's heart in twenty minutes. Big barrels, deep chests, tremendous lungs and strong quarters — horses don't come no better for this kind of country, for mountain fighting! And the proof of that's what the Nez Perce did!"

He was a horseman, all right; his eyes were glowing.

"Last spring, the government voided its treaties with the Nez Perce. It told Joseph and his band they'd have to give up their home valley and come into the mission at Lapwai with the Christian Injuns! Joseph was mad as hell, but he finally agreed. Only, before they could get their stock rounded up, some of his young men went on a tear and killed some whites — "

"They killed some men," Sundance said thinly, "who'd bushwhacked their fathers and their brothers — "

"It don't make a damn what those men did. They were white, and that tore it. Joseph ran, and the Army took out after him."

Drury's big chest swelled. "Sundance, I was in the war, Fifth Michigan cavalry, and I know horse soldiers. Nobody, no cavalry in the world has ever done what the Nez Perce did. Every time the Army caught up with 'em, they fought it to a standstill! They led the soldiers on a chase all over the north-west, sixteen hundred miles; they crossed the Lolo Trail over the Bitterroots, men, women, children, the whole tribe, the trail so rough our cavalry couldn't follow. It was their horses that made that possible. They were tryin' to get to Canada and join Sittin' Bull and his Hunkpapa Sioux up there, and they almost made it. They were only forty miles from the border when General Miles cornered 'em. It was cold and snowin' and he had artillery and the Indians hadn't had a chance to hunt — Even so, they fought for five days before Joseph surrendered. But before he did, the prime stallions and mares of the Nez Perce herd, their best breeding stock, vanished."

Memories too recent and raw rose up in Sundance. Suddenly he was back in the camp on the bend of Snake Creek, shrapnel bursting overhead, women and children screaming, a whole family just buried alive by an artillery shell exploding directly on their front. While men tried desperately to dig them out, he had wriggled up to where Thunder Rolling in the Mountains, whom white men called Chief Joseph, lay with his rifle out before him and his stocky body swathed in a tattered blanket. Rifle fire snapped and whacked above their heads, the roar of guns was continuous.

"Thunder," Sundance yelled. "I want to go out to Sitting Bull. I can make it in three days. I can bring back three hundred Sioux. Can you hold out that long?"

"I can if I want all my people killed," Chief Joseph shouted. He was about Sundance's age, but he looked a decade older from the weight of the responsibility laid upon him. Looking Glass and Yellow Wolf and Jim Sundance were his fighting chiefs

— Sundance had spent years among the Nez Perce, had been adopted into the tribe, had status almost as high as Joseph's own — but the responsibility for making policy lay on Joseph alone. A bullet snarled above their heads and both ducked . . . "There is no hope. To save the women and the children, I must surrender." He started to say something else, but his words were drowned in the roar of an exploding artillery shell. Somewhere within their fortress in the creek's bend, a woman screamed and a child bawled, and both sounds were cut off sharply, as the people who made them died.

"You see?" Joseph said bitterly in the silence that followed. It lingered, almost eerily, in that bleak fortress in the mountains, with snow drifting down and the air bone-crushing cold.

Sundance looked toward the American lines not far away. The Seventh Cavalry, with a grudge to repay, the Fifth, elements of infantry, and that damned artillery. And Miles in command, and Sundance knew Nelson Miles. He was no truly great Indian fighter like George Crook, but he had learned something important about fighting Indians in the Northwest; once the snows set in, and Indians could not pitch their teepees nor hunt buffalo, they could not carry on war, either. Especially against cannons. Sundance felt in his throat the bitter knowledge, like a stinging bile, that Joseph was right.

"I will have to make the best peace I can," said Joseph.

"Then I'll help you."

"No." The chief turned toward him, eyes hard. "No, you must not stay here."

"But — "

The silence held. Joseph's words were clear in the cold air. "You are no ordinary Indian, and no ordinary Nez Perce. You know the white man's ways and the white man's laws and can speak to the Grandfather in Washington who has sent these people against us — "

He broke off as a stray bullet dug into the dirt of the gully used as a trench in which they were crouched. "Besides," he went on coolly in a moment, "we are only Indians, but you are half white and a former Army scout. If they take us, we will live. But if they take you, they will hang you as a traitor."

"I'm not afraid of that!"

"I am," said Joseph. "If you die, who is to stand for us before the Grandfather in Washington, to whom we must surrender? You have a voice there, we have none. Whatever happens, you must stay alive and be behind us to help us when we need it in ways we cannot see now." He paused. "Sundance, my mind is clear. I will not see more women and more children killed. I shall talk to Miles. But before I do, you must leave — "

"Joseph, my friend — "

"And take the horses with you," Joseph said.

Bullets began to crack and splatter. Peering over the edge of the gully, Sundance caught occasional flashes of blue; he heated the barrel of his Winchester firing at them. Ducking, cramming new rounds into the weapon, he caught Joseph's words.

"The horses," Joseph said. "If you do not save them, the breeders, the Army will take them. Maybe, after we give up, they will send us back to the mountains, to our home, at least to Lapwai. Then you can bring the horses to us."

In his handsome face, his eyes lit. "But the horses must be saved! The stallions and the mares to carry on the Appaloosa line, not the bad line at Lapwai, but the high mountain stock! Sundance, you must take the horses out!"

"Thunder — "

Joseph looked steadily at him. "I will have no argument. You will take Two Trees and Dead Man Walking, and tonight when it is dark you will

37

leave, with the stallions and the best mares. You will take them and hide them somewhere and leave Two Trees and Dead Man Walking to guard them. Later, if we still live, when we know where we will be and what will happen to us, I'll write you in the white man's way at Fort Laramie and tell you what to do with the horses." He paused. "Sundance, you're Cheyenne, but you are also adopted Nez Perce. You know us, you know that our horses are our life. What I entrust you with is the life of the Nez Perce people, all we have left. In the name of *Wyakin*, do what I say, for the sake of the *Tsutpeli*, The People . . ."

Sundance saw the pleading in Chief Joseph's eyes, and he nodded. "All right. I'll take them out tonight and find a place to hide them."

"Yes. And no one must know where, not even I. There must be no way for the soldiers to get such information out of me or any of my people. They may torture us, or later we may be starving,

38

hungry enough to sell our heritage. But we cannot if we do not know where you put the horses . . ."

"All right," Sundance said. Then he ducked as another shell burst overhead . . .

"Like I was sayin'," Drury went on as Sundance snapped back to awareness, "you couldn't stay out of an Indian fight like that Nez Perce war. The indians at Leavenworth and Lapwai both have talked. The Army knows you were there and it knows you took six fine Nez Perce stallions and twenty-five mares and got 'em out before the surrender. What it don't know is where."

"That's too bad," Sundance said.

Luke Drury's face darkened. "All right, Sundance, there'll be no more beatin' around the bush. The Army didn't send Joseph back to the Northwest, it loaded him and his people on flatboats and sent 'em south. They're mountain Indians and they'll never make it down in Kansas, they'll die off like flies. But I'll tell you this right now, they don't have a prayer of goin' home again unless the Army gits their breedin' stock."

His eyes glittered in his leathery face. "What the Army captured was only worn-out culls. There's Appaloosas at Lapwai, too, but they're like coyotes compared to wolves, stacked up against Joseph's horses. The Army wants those stallions, Sundance, to breed up their remounts for the rough country up here, and you'd better get it through your head right now that it's not gonna take 'no' for an answer."

Sundance said, "Do you represent the Army? You speak for it officially?"

"Let's just say that I know what the Army wants and I've got a lot freer hand to git it for 'em." His lips pulled back slightly from his teeth. "Let's say that I can do business in my own way and be a lot rougher than the Army without stirrin' up any fuss, if it comes to that. But the Army's there, Sundance, it's behind me, and you can't fight it. It's too big even for you."

Sundance did not speak. He knew, though, exactly what Drury meant and did not doubt it for an instant. He knew, too, that never would Joseph consent to selling the Nez Perce stud to the very people who would use the Appaloosas to keep the Nez Perce in subjection.

He shook his head. "Sorry, Drury. No deal."

Drury carefully laid both hands on the table. "Listen, Sundance. We know why you came to Deadwood. Joseph sent you — to meet somebody here who wanted to buy the horses. If you could get the right price, you were to go ahead and sell. In fact, we know everything. The man you were supposed to meet was from England, his name was Sir John Bucknell, and when he got the Appaloosas, he was to ship them home to England. Well, the American Army's not gonna let that happen. It's gonna keep those horses here, not see 'em go into the service of a foreign power. But we're being reasonable, Sundance. We — I — am prepared to pay you twenty thousand dollars for the Appaloosas, five thousand down right now and fifteen thousand when you turn 'em over to my men. Twenty thousand dollars, Sundance that's a lot of money."

Sundance only shrugged. "It could be double that, Drury, and I wouldn't sell you the horses. Not unless Joseph told me to. And I know him well enough to know that he won't." He nodded. "Your information's good. Yeah, I'm meeting Bucknell here, and if his price is right, he gets the stallions. And only him, nobody else. So go back to Sheridan or whoever sent you and tell them — "

He broke off. A slow, humorless grin was spreading across Drury's face. "Sundance," Drury said and shook his head. "You won't make no deal with Bucknell."

Sundance sat up straight. "No?"

"Not unless they got banks in hell." Drury's grin widened. "Sundance, Sir John Bucknell's dead."

# 3

SOMEHOW, Jim Sundance felt no surprise. What he did feel, sitting there immobile, staring into Drury's mocking face, was rage.

But his voice was soft. "Well, that's convenient for you and the Army, ain't it?"

"You might say so. After all, Bucknell was a greenhorn. He should have known better than to walk around Deadwood after dark. Somebody shot him in the back and took his money. That kind of thing happens every day in a town like this."

Sundance said quietly, "All right, Drury. I'll grant it does. But it don't help you one bit, or the Army either. It just means you and me both had long rides for nothin'. Zero for me, zero for you, zero for Joseph, and zero for the Army." His voice sharpened. "So you go on back to Oregon and forget the Nez Perce horses."

"I don't forget anything!" Drury's voice crackled. "One way or the other, we aim to have those horses." He pushed back his chair. "Okay, Sundance, I'm givin' you one last chance. Twenty thousand and we make the deal right now. Otherwise — "

"Otherwise what?" Sundance almost whispered.

Drury stood up, towering, thickbodied, hands close to his guns. "Otherwise," he rasped, "I reckon I'll have to beat some sense into your half breed head with a gun barrel. I — "

His hand moved and Sundance turned the table over.

The rage in him now was like dynamite exploding. He could not contain it and his knees came up and hit the table and it slammed into Drury and Drury staggered back, and that gave Sundance the leeway he needed. He came off the chair against the wall, and as Drury wheeled, right hand swooping instinctively for his gun, Sundance, laughing, furious, hit him.

The halfbreed's big fist caught Drury squarely between the eyes. It was like hitting a brick wall. Sundance was already following with a blow to Drury's gut, but the big man whirled aside, and Sundance's fist missed by a quarter of an inch, and Drury laughed and said, "That way, eh?" and hit Sundance in the temple. Sundance was picked up by the blow's force and slammed across the room until another table caught him. He shook a ringing head, blurred vision cleared, and he saw Drury, laughing once more, coming at him, great fists clubbed.

Sundance snorted and came off the table. He weaved aside, and Drury's left missed and Sundance hit Drury low, halfway between gut and kidney, pivoted, and as Drury turned, off balance, smashed Drury's nose with a cross-over right. Bone went beneath his knuckles, and Drury howled, and suddenly Drury's chin and chest were covered with flowing scarlet. Sundance hit Drury again, an up-chopping blow deliberately designed to rip the flesh by Drury's eye; it succeeded; Drury rocked back, bleeding from yet another wound, and Sundance gave him no mercy, came in fast. His next blow smashed Drury's mouth. An old strategy and always effective, cut the soft parts, hurt the face and get the blood to running, send the victim into panic. Then he was easy meat.

But it didn't work with Drury. He backed away from Sundance, keeping fists up, shook his head violently, slinging blood, cleared his vision. Something clicked in Sundance's head, suddenly he knew he had met maybe the toughest opponent he'd ever faced. Because neither blood nor pain was scaring Drury. Again he shook his head and more blood flew, and then Drury came after Sundance, and for so big a man he was like a feather on his feet.

All right, Sundance thought. So it was going to be a fight. He laughed softly, not dismayed, and he and Drury came together.

Everybody in the room was watching now, from a safe distance. It was like the collision of two savage bull buffalo on the prairie. Bottles jingled on the shelves behind the bar and men drew in breaths of awe as Sundance and Drury, at close range, pounded each other savagely for a moment, neither feeling hurt, each only wanting to deal it. Drury smashed Sundance's mouth this time and hit Sundance just below the rib cage, and then caught Sundance with a hammering right to the side of the head, but in the meantime Sundance had chopped three fierce blows into Drury's gut and some of the breath and steam went out of the man. That was why the head blow did not kill Sundance; otherwise it might have.

As it was, it knocked Sundance down, and Drury, inches taller and pounds heavier and scarlet to his waist, was still on his feet, and he bellowed laughter and ran towards Sundance and kicked out. Sundance rolled, but the boot caught him on the thigh. He rolled again, beneath a table, as Drury kicked at his head and Drury's other boot missed, and then Drury had picked up the table and thrown it aside, but Sundance was boiling up. The table crashed somewhere behind them, and as Drury clenched his hands again, Sundance hit him on the very point of the jaw with all the rising weight of arm and body.

He felt the blow vibrate through his whole being. Drury staggered back, stunned, as any human would have to be. Sundance came after him, panting, hit him again in the same place. The right blow there would drop any man, no matter how strong or tough; but he had not landed the right blow yet. Drury shook his head, hit Sundance glancingly on the shoulder, then brought up an amazing quick knee toward Sundance's groin.

Sundance turned, caught it on his

thigh, recovered balance and hit Drury on the jaw again, and then again, as Drury pounded him on the head and shoulders. The sound of the blows was like a strong axeman chopping wood. Drury's head rocked back and sideways; suddenly the blows took effect.

"Jesus," Drury said, or something that sounded like it. All at once his knees sagged. Sundance angled the next blow, snapped Drury's head around with it.

Drury's eyes went blank. He raised a hand, dropped it as if it weighed a ton. Then he lurched to one knee. Sundance hit him again and Drury sprawled on the floor, a sodden bloody mass, making a rasping sound through his battered nose and mouth.

Sundance stood over him, bleeding also, begining to hurt, but feeling a wild triumph. "Drury!" he shouted.

Drury managed to raise his head, shielding it with a weak hand, made a sound.

"You tell 'em!" Sundance roared.

50

"You hear? You tell Sheridan and you tell all of 'em! I'll never give 'em the Nez Perce horses to breed up their remounts to fight other Indians! I'll kill the goddamn stud first if I can't sell it somewhere else! You hear? You tell 'em that!"

Drury moaned something. He made a move Sundance did not like and Sundance bent painfully, pulled Drury's Colts from holster, slung them across the room.

"You tell 'em, damn you," he rasped, wiping blood from his own face on his buckskin sleeve. Then, on legs that wobbled, he backed out of the saloon.

Drury lay where he had fallen as Sundance shoved through the doors. They made a clattering sound. Sundance was on the sidewalk. Eagle, the Appaloosa stallion, scented his blood and snorted.

Sundance unlatched the reins of the big, strangely spotted horse, swung up on the right side, Indian style. At a heel signal, the horse backed, and Sundance watched the saloon doors for a moment. No one came through them. Then Sundance wheeled the horse, kicked it gently, and it went galloping through the deep mud down the Deadwood gulch.

Dark spruce boughs formed a canopy over Jim Sundance as, in a fern-bedded forest; he knelt beside a rivulet of icy water, sponging blood from his face. The cold liquid helped kill pain, but he would have a puffy lip for a day or two.

No one had interfered with him as he had ridden out of town. Clear of Deadwood, he had turned off on a trail he knew of old, one that had taken him through a notch in the hills away from the main road. Now, sitting by the swift-running creek on his spread-out blankets, he dried his face, made a cigarette and lit it.

He had some thinking to do, but first he must check his weapons. There was no doubt whatsoever in his mind that he would need them soon, all of them.

The Colt and the Winchester were easily taken care of, fieldstripped, cleaned, oiled, and, fully loaded, ready for action. Meanwhile, Eagle, the stallion, grazed nearby, unpicketed, unhobbled, ready to come at either a whistle or a slight clicking sound Sundance might make in his throat, a summons which could be given in secrecy. More than that, the big horse also served as watchdog; his nostrils and his ears would catch the approach of anyone long before even Sundance's keen senses.

When he was satisfied with the guns, Sundance pulled to himself the two big panniers that had been tied behind the saddle cantle. One was long, cylindrical; the other shaped almost like a big disc. He opened the long one first, and very carefully removed the things it contained.

First he withdrew a short, recurved

bow of juniper wood, tipped at its ends with notched bits of buffalo horn. He stroked it carefully, searching for any split, found none. His fingers examined as meticulously the string made from the back sinews of a buffalo cow, and it was all right. He strung the bow, pulled it experimentally. That took a lot of strength. He could send an arrow more than three hundred yards with this weapon, or, as he had done more than once, put one clean through a bull buffalo, or, for that matter, a man. It was a fine weapon, the first he had ever learned to use, and it had one great advantage over a rifle: the ability to kill from a distance with no flash, report, or powdersmoke to betray from where its missile came.

He unstrung it, put it aside, then took the quiver from the *parfleche*. It held more than two dozen arrows, and Sundance took them from the panther-skin case, which still had the tail attached, and examined every one. Each was long and absolutely straight and the feathers, black, strong, durable, taken from vulture's wings, were in order. Their points were barbed and razor sharp, some of hard flint and others of obsidian, black volcanic glass. In this era, that was unusual. Most Indians who still used bows nowadays preferred arrowpoints of iron. Sundance, however, stuck to the stone ones, which he chipped himself, meticulously working off flake after flake with a tool made from a notched elk-antler prong. The extra effort was worth it in his estimation: a stone arrowpoint made a much more grievous wound in flesh, had greater shocking power, and was nearly impossible to remove once imbeded. The way he lived, that was an advantage that was important.

When the arrows had been restored to their quiver, he drew from the pannier a small roll of otterskin and sat for a moment holding it in his hands. This was his medicine bag, and it held things that were sacred to him; it held his luck. The fact that he was still alive after all he'd been through was pragmatic proof to him of its power; as he held it, memories surged into his mind. He seemed to see once again a Cheyenne camp in the old days, the good days before the white men came, when the Cheyennes were still lords of the high prairie between the Rockies and the Black Hills. He saw ring after ring of teepees arranged in the sacred circle, horse herds that covered miles of plains, smelled the mingled smoke of burning wood and buffalo chips with sweetgrass laid in the fire to perfume it; he seemed to hear again the beating of drums, the chant of dancing Dog Soldiers, the most powerful and feared warrior society of any tribe . . . For a moment, longing washed over him in a wave, and then came the bitterness. Those days were gone, vanished in a single decade. The Indians were no longer free, only prisoners on squalid, arid reservations far from home. Joseph had been the last, the very last . . .

Sundance laid aside the medicine pouch, and then from the pannier carefully withdrew a folded war-bonnet encased in a muslin cover. Unsheathing it, he shook it out. Richly beaded and quilled at the headband, its bright eagle feathers fell into proper place, dozens of them, each earned the hard way in his youth by counting coup and officially awarded in council. Each conjured up its own memory of an enemy touched in combat while still alive, another killed, a successful horse-stealing expedition, a grizzly bear brought down with bow and arrow or lance . . . He folded the bonnet, put it back in its sheath. He had not worn it since last year during those nearly six months with the Nez Perce. Maybe he would never have the chance to wear it again.

After that, he opened the other pannier, the round one. The main thing in it was his shield. Gently he took it out, careful never to let it touch the ground, for the shield was luck, too, like the medicine bag, and if it touched the ground its luck was gone and it would have to be reconsecrated in an intricate ceremony. It was maybe a yard or a little less in diameter, made of thick buffalo neck hide stretched tight over a juniper frame, a padding of grass, antelope skin pulled over that. Decorated with a thunderbird, it would stop an arrow, even turn an old-fashioned musket ball, but it would not stop modern ammunition. From it, as Drury had said, dangled six tufts of hair, three black, one blond, one brown, one red. They had come from the heads of the murderers of his parents; they were the last scalps he had ever taken, but he would not give these up.

Carefully, he replaced the shield and closed the pannier. Picking up the bow, he strung it, slipped the quiver over his shoulder. Leaving the horse to guard his other gear, he moved away through the woods, making absolutely no sound. He had not gone far before a bird fluttered up out of a clump of fern to perch on the lower branch of a spruce: a grouse, the stupid kind called a fool hen that seemed to have no fear of man. Sundance nocked an arrow to the bow, drew the feather to his cheekbone, let the shaft fly. The small obsidian point neatly severed the bird's head; it came fluttering down and, without any noise to betray his hiding place, he had his supper.

Retrieving the arrow, he went back to the creek and built a fire on bone-dry squaw wood from the lower branches of the forest. Almost smokeless, it quickly built a bed of coals while he dressed the fool hen and rolled it in clay. Letting it bake, he leaned back against his saddle and thought about Drury and Bucknell and the Nez Perce horses.

Maybe, he thought, he had been too hasty, too edgy. But Drury had rubbed him the wrong way from the start, and then the news of Bucknell's death . . . And the fact that Drury made no secret that the Army backed him, that it was the Army that really wanted the Nez Perce horses . . . Sundance understood the Army very well. He knew that it could not spend the money directly itself, twenty thousand for a handful of Indian ponies, as the press would call them if it found out. But it could easily guarantee a remount contractor far more than that in business if he would guarantee to get them and breed from them. Over the years, Drury would make far more than twenty thousand from the spotted stallions and their mares: he would make a fortune. Worse than that, the cavalry would use those very horses to keep the Indians who had bred them in subjection . . . Anyhow, it was no wonder that Drury was so hellbent to get those horses. He was playing for high stakes, damned high stakes. Sundance did not think a beating in a fist fight would stop him, either.

Of course, if the Army really wanted Appaloosas, they were available at Lapwai. But the ones owned by the Christian Indians there were from a degraded line, their best stock sold off over the years. Only the Joseph horses were the old, pure strain, and surely by now every mare would have dropped a foal. Sundance had intended beginning the bargaining with the Englishman at no less then forty thousand dollars — Eagle, the stallion, snorted.

Jim Sundance was on his feet in an instant. The big horse had swung to point his muzzle down the stream, head up, ears pricked forward. In the distance, there was the faint click of shod hooves on rock. Sundance grabbed bow, arrows, Winchester. One moment he was there, on his blankets; the next he had simply disappeared, melting soundlessly into the shadows of the big trees. Thirty yards from camp, he found cover, a big log, and threw himself behind it. From here he could command the clearing and watch the horse as well. He drew an arrow, strung the bow, waited. It could, of course, be Drury or someone hired by him, but he did not think so. These riders came too openly. Nevertheless, he would take no chances.

Now he saw motion between the trees. Then there were two riders coming single file, following a game trail along the water straight toward his camp. Sundance could not see who they were as yet for the screening brush, but in a moment they'd come into the open, into the clearing where his saddle and blankets still lay and Eagle stood tensely.

Then they were there, reining in their mounts, staring at his gear. Sundance frowned and, surprised, eased the bowstring.

The rider on a spotted horse wore a dirty sombrero, a greasy buckskin shirt, and corduroy pants tucked into boots, as well as a Colt around the waist. But the high-pitched twanging voice as she called out, "Jim? Jim Sundance, whur are you?" was a woman's.

Sundance materialized from behind the log, and both riders were startled when he appeared at the clearing's edge. "Hello, Calamity," he said.

Calamity Jane Canary, in man's clothes, was in her late forties or early fifties and ugly as home made sin. But the other woman with her was not. She was young and lovely, with hair the color of hammered gold beneath an absurd little hat, her eyes were huge and green, vivid in her pale ivory face, and, unlike Jane Canary, she rode sidesaddle, a black velvet dress modeling a figure tall and fully curved.

Now she raked those magnificent eyes over Sundance, from the yellow hair down to the moccasins, and something flickered in them. When she spoke, it was with a musical English accent.

"How do you do, Mr. Sundance," she said. "I am Lady Doris Bucknell. My late husband was the man you came to Deadwood to meet. They've murdered him, but I intend to carry on in his stead. I want to talk to you about the Nez Perce horses."

It had never occured to Jim Sundance that any man in his right mind would bring his wife to Deadwood, but, of course, Sir John Bucknell had had no idea of what he was getting into. Only faintly surprised, Sundance touched his hat brim. "Lady Bucknell. I'm sorry about your husband." He gave her a hand and, lithely, she came off the big horse, landing close enough to Sundance so that he caught the odor of her perfume.

Calamity Jane swung down. "You see, Miz Bucknell? I told you, Jim Sundance's a a real gentleman, jest like my late dear friend Wild Bill. A wild one in a fight, but he knows how to treat a lady." She gave a raucous laugh. "Jim, that shore was a sweet beatin' you handed that big coyote Drury back in Carl Mann's. It was a full half hour before he come out of it, and likely the doctor's still workin' on that nose and eye of his. Only — " her laugh died. "You shoulda killed him, that's what you oughta done. He's bad medicine, Jim, I can spot his kind a long way off. You ain't through with him yet. You shoulda blowed a hole in him right off, like Wild Bill would have done."

"I agree with Jane," Doris Bucknell said with unexpected sharpness. "You should have shot him, Mr. Sundance."

Sundance looked at the two women. "What do you know about Drury, both of you?"

"All I know," Jane said, "is that him and his men been stompin' around Deadwood for the past two weeks like they owned the town."

"His men?"

"He's been puttin' together a crew, hirin' some pretty tough characters, Jim. They was all out of town today on some kind of errand for him, or you'd had a lot more music to dance to than you did. 'Course, if they'd ganged up on you, I'da took a hand myself." She touched her gun butt. "Anyhow, he rubs me the wrong way. I was shore glad to see you hand him one.

And when Lady Bucknell come to me later and asked if I could find out whur you'd gone and bring her to you, I said shore. I knowed you'd head for water and that we'd find you up one creek or another." She gave that crowing laugh. "I'm glad I ain't Drury, or I got a hunch I'd have one of them Cheyenne arrows clear through my gut."

"You might have had," Sundance said. He turned to Doris Bucknell, gesturing toward his grounded saddle. "Maybe you'd like to sit down, Lady Bucknell, and tell me what you know about Drury, and then we'll get down to business."

"Of course." He liked the way that she seemed as at ease in this forest clearing as in a drawing room. He supposed she was not much older than twenty-five, and she had been through a lot in a strange place, and yet she still had obvious reserves of strength. She was, Sundance thought, a real thoroughbred herself.

For a moment her face was touched

66

by grief as she looked into the fire's coals. "My husband was one of the most famous horsemen of the British Empire. Horses were his passion. He served in the Bengal Lancers on the Northern Frontier of India and — racing, polo, hunting, he loved them all. For that matter, so do I.

"Anyhow," she continued, "our newspapers were full of the story of your magnificent Nez Perce Indians last year, and their great retreat. There was much about the horses, too, and one day at breakfast John simply decided that he absolutely had to have a stud of Appaloosas. So, quite simply, he decided we were coming to America to buy them. That was the way he was."

They had, she said, come directly to the miserable Quapaw Reserve in Kansas, where the Nez Perce were jammed in with the Modocs, also sent down from the Northwest after an earlier war. "We were disappointed at first. They were so shabby and so dirty and their horse were only nags . . . "

67

"Well, everything they had was taken." Iron rang in Sundance's voice. "You should have seen them before, up in the mountains, when they were free . . ."

"Yes, I would like to have seen that. At any rate, we almost turned around and went home; there seemed nothing for us. Then we heard rumors — about the Nez Perce horses saved during the last battle with the Army . . . and about the man who saved them." Her eyes met Sundance's.

"It took a long time to win the confidence of Chief Joseph," she went on, "but John finally did it. He promised Joseph to pay whatever you should ask, and promised that the horses would be taken out of the country so that the Army could not get them and use them against the Nez Perce or other Indians. He met all of Joseph's conditions, and then Joseph wrote you to meet us here in Deadwood. It was all supposed to be very secret, but apparently it wasn't."

"You can bet it wasn't," Sundance said. "The Army had spies planted in Joseph's band. Nez Perce, especially starving ones, can be bought like anybody else. So they made a deal with Drury . . . "

"To kill my husband," she said bitterly.

"Not necessarily. Just to get the horses. Likely they left it up to him to do it in his own way."

"All I know," Doris Bucknell said, "is that Drury was almost the first person we met in Deadwood. We had no idea anyone even knew we were there, but he came to our hotel room immediately and he made no bones about it. He said that he knew our mission, that we were wasting our time, and that when you came, you would deal with no one but him. And that if we persisted, we would find ourselves in deep trouble. He warned John to leave Deadwood right away or take the consequences."

Her voice was hard. "My husband

69

was a brave man and not one to mince words. He told Drury, quite simply, to go to hell. After that, he always carried a gun wherever he went. But what good is a gun against someone who shoots you in the back? Now — " she raised her head " — he's dead, buried in this dreadful place ten thousand miles from home! But I'll avenge him, Mr. Sundance! I have the money to buy the Nez Perce horses, and I shall certainly have them!"

Sundance drew in a long breath. "Does Drury know how you feel?"

"He surely does. He came to me at the funeral, crying crocodile tears, actually trying to find out what I intended to do. I told him I intended to carry out John's mission. Then his whole attitude changed. Now it was me he threatened. He told me I had better not stick around, as he put it. He said Deadwood could be rough on women as well as men." She smiled savagely. "I told him what John had told him — that is, to go to hell. And then I walked away. That was last week, Mr. Sundance. Now, do you understand why I wish you had killed him?"

Jim Sundance nodded slowly. "It's beginning to look like I may have to, sooner or later, anyhow."

"That's th' boy, Jim!" Calamity slapped her thigh.

Lady Bucknell looked at her. "Jane, perhaps you would excuse us . . . "

"Shore. I know ye wanta talk business. Well, I got a piece of a bottle in my saddle bags. I'll jest go up the creek and have a leetle dram." She strode away. Lady Bucknell looked after her with a faint smile. "She's been very kind to me," she said. Then, seriously, she turned to Sundance.

"Very well, Mr. Sundance. What are you asking for the horses?"

"Forty thousand dollars for the six studs, the twenty-five mares, and whatever new foals they've dropped in the past year, delivered to the railhead."

Doris Bucknell's brows went up.

"Forty thousand dollars? Eight thousand pounds? Isn't that rather dear for a band of Indian ponies?"

Sundance pointed to Eagle. "That's one of your Indian ponies, Lady Bucknell. Look him over if you'd like to. There are better stallions than him in the bunch. You know perfectly well you can sell the stallions alone for that much in England, or certainly earn back the money in stud fees. And that doesn't count the value of the mares and foals."

She arose and walked to where Eagle grazed. Sundance spoke to the big horse, and he let her come to him, run hands over his head and muzzle, down his neck, along the line of loin and rump. She felt the strong legs, and Sundance knew that her boast was not an empty one: she *was* a horsewoman. When she straightened up, her face was glowing, her eyes shining.

"Better than he? Incredible!"

"But true."

"Then your terms are met," she said.

"Twenty thousand now and twenty thousand when they're loaded on the railroad cars. Right?"

"Right." Sundance felt a vast relief; he had not failed Joseph after all.

"I'll give you a certified draft on a New York bank this afternoon. Then — when can we start after the horses?"

Sundance stared at her. Standing there in her blue velvet riding habit, with Eagle in the background, she might have been a Currier and Ives print; she was very beautiful, and something within him responded to that. But he shook his head.

"*We?*"

"Of course. I intend to go with you when you get them. You don't think I'll stay in a place like Deadwood waiting for you?"

"No need for you to. You go on to Omaha or St. Louis and I'll bring the horses there."

"Oh, no, Mr. Sundance." Her voice was determined. "I'll pay you the first twenty thousand this afternoon, and

73

with that much invested, I intend to make sure there are no slip-ups. It's not that I don't trust you, but those horses are more to me than just horses now. They are the symbol of my revenge against John's killer. They are a memorial to my husband, and I want to see them as soon as possible and be with them all the way."

Sundance kept his voice even. "I understand how you feel. The fact remains that those horses are in a place that nobody can reach without a long, hard ride. I've got 'em hidden in mountains that make these Black Hills look like warts, and the way in is a trip that not many men could make, much less a woman. Besides, there's still Drury and the Army. They'll do everything they can to get their hands on the Nez Perce stud, and I'll probably have to fight before I get 'em to the railhead." He smiled, to take the sting out of his refusal. "You wait in Omaha, and I'll be in there with 'em in a couple of months."

"I shall not!" Doris Bucknell's eyes flared. "I may not be a Westerner, Mr. Sundance, but I was brought up on horseback and in the hunting field. I can ride anything with four legs anywhere you or anyone else can go! And I can shoot, too: my father served in India also, and he taught me how to use a rifle and pistol while we were there. I won't hamper you, I promise, but I must go with you!"

"No. It's out of the question."

"Then our deal is off."

Sundance looked at her a moment. "Suit yourself," he said coldly and turned away.

"Mr. Sundance!"

He took his time about facing her again.

Her mouth worked, and her eyes were angry. "Very well. I suppose I have no choice but to yield. I'll wait for you in Omaha, then, and you'll bring the animals to me there."

"That's better," Sundance said, taking no pleasure in his triumph. It was a matter of necessity. He thought of the narrow, dizzying trail across cliffs almost sheer, of the dangerous river crossings. When he had hidden those horses, he had chosen the most inaccessible spot he knew; and it would be a gruelling, dangerous journey even for himself.

"I suppose it is. All the same, I wish — " She shrugged. "Well, shall we go into Deadwood and transfer the money?"

"Right." Sundance raked aside the coals, brought out the ball of mud. "First, try some fool hen *a la* Cheyenne Indian. Then we'll head for town."

This time Sundance did not ride boldly up the main street of Deadwood. Instead, he sent Calamity Jane on ahead to scout the town while he and Doris Bucknell took a circuitous path through the forest on the walls of the mountain above the town. When, from a hiding place in the brush, they could look down on the gulch and its scattered buildings, they waited. Presently Jane appeared, coming up almost as silently as Sundance himself could have, for she'd been on the frontier a long time, and when she could bring her raddled senses to bear, she knew the tricks of the scout's trade. "Drury's up and around. He's bandaged all over that ugly mug of his, but I reckon there's plenty of fight left in him. Didn't see nothin' of his men, though. Guess they're still out of town."

"Maybe," Sundance said. Holding Eagle tight-reined, he thought for a moment. "I'm not the one in danger so much," he said. "Not right now. Drury knows that if he kills me, nobody will ever see those horses again. But you — " He looked at Doris Bucknell. "You're the one he'd like to see out of the way. His only competition. Once he sees us ride into town together, he'll know exactly what's going on. And . . ."

"You think he'd really kill me?"

"I don't think he'd even blink an

eye. Over the years, the stud fees from those stallions and the remounts he can sell to the Army could mean more than a hundred thousand dollars to him. People have been killed out here, women included, for a lot less. Maybe we should ride on. We can go on up to Custer or to Rapid City, it doesn't have to be Deadwood. It would be a lot safer for you."

"No," Doris Bucknell said. "I don't want to waste even an hour, much less days, in getting this thing under way. I insist we ride down now, go to the bank, handle the whole thing and have it over with. Then I'll catch the stage east tomorrow and you'll be free to go get the horses without more delay."

"I don't like to take the chance," Sundance said. "You don't know how a man like Drury works. He could rig a gunfight on the street, for instance, and you'd stop a stray bullet . . . Or maybe break into your hotel room at night — "

"All the same . . . " Doris began,

78

and then she smiled. "Wait a minute, Mr. Sundance. Jane — " She leaned close to Calamity and whispered. Jane Canary's rugged face looked startled, then broke into a grin.

"Sho!" she crowed, and without another word to Sundance, she and Doris Bucknell turned their horses and rode into deeper brush.

"Hold on — " Sundance began, but it was useless. They were already gone. He heard them halt their mounts, and he tipped back his hat, hooked one leg over the saddle horn, and rolled a cigarette. If, he thought, he could get the twenty thousand this afternoon, he could send it immediately to his man in Washington. He and Barbara would see to it that it got to Joseph at once, safely, and was put to proper use.

Barbara . . . Sundance felt something stir within him. Barbara Colfax, Two Roads Woman, her Cheyenne name was. Years before, she had been captured by the Cheyennes, adopted into the tribe. Sundance had taken her from the Indians, but of her own free will she had returned, for she had fallen in love with the wild, free life of the horsemen of the high plains. She had fallen in love with Jim Sundance, too, and had become his woman.

But now the Cheyennes were broken and on reservations and Two Roads Woman was in Washington, working for the cause of the Indians there, and it had been a long time, many months, since they had seen one another, since he had held her in his arms. It would be months more before he saw her again. But that could not be helped. He had too much work to do out here, and she had too much there. Each was equally important in its own way; like this matter of the Nez Perce horses, there were still rear-guard battles to be fought, desperate efforts to salvage anything possible from the wreckage of what had once been an Indian empire.

Still, he wished — Then he heard the horses coming from the brush, and he turned. For a moment, disbelievingly, he stared. Then, suddenly, as the figure in the battered sombrero and dirty buckskin shirt tipped back the hat and smiled, he understood.

"How do you like me as a frontierswoman, Jim Sundance?" Doris Bucknell asked. She hitched at the revolver around her waist and gave a pale imitation of Calamity Jane spitting, and Jane Canary, dressed now in Doris' riding habit, laughed. "Fer that matter, ain't I purty gorgeous, myself?" Then she sobered. "Sundance, if Lady Bucknell keeps that hat pulled down and rides my hawss, ain't no reason why she can't ride in with you and be fair to middlin' safe, at least until she comes outa the bank. Then you git her to her hotel quick and pen her in so Drury's folks can't git to her and stay there and watch her. I'll meet you later on and we'll swap clothes again."

Sundance ran his eyes over Doris Bucknell again. She was mounted on Jane's animal, riding now astride in the long-stirruped way of the frontier American. Jane's clothes were baggy enough to hide the lines of her figure, and as she pulled the hat down again, Sundance nodded.

"Okay, we'll give it a try. Jane, when you come in, don't try to pretend you're Lady Bucknell, or you might catch a slug yourself. Ride in with your head up so they can see who you are. Doris — " the first name came out involuntarily " — you slouch down and don't look around. And if I say ride, you hit that horse with spurs and take off with all he's got. Because that'll mean there'll be trouble with guns. Don't worry, I'll cover you."

Doris Bucknell touched the butt of the Colt. "I told you, I can handle this — "

"Honey," Jane Canary said firmly, "you do exactly what Jim Sundance says. He's been in the trouble business a real long time."

"Oh, very well . . . "

"Now," said Jane, "y'all ride on

down, and good luck. I'll see you later. Oh, hold on. One thing more, Lady Bucknell." She rode up alongside Doris's mount, reached in the saddle bag and pulled out a whiskey bottle. "Might as well have a little jolt or two while I'm waitin' . . . "

Doris Bucknell laughed. Then she said, "Come on, Jim." She too used the first name easily. And she followed close behind Sundance as he put the Appaloosa down the slope toward Deadwood.

# 4

WINDING down a precipitous skein of trails past occasional cabins on the mountainside, presently they reached the town, coming out almost directly behind the heavy-walled log building that was the bank. Rounding its corner, Sundance rode tensely, hand close to his Colt. Behind him, Doris kept her head bent and the hat pulled well over her eyes. Her golden hair was tucked up under it without a lock escaping.

"All right," Sundance said, satisfied the coast was clear. He swung down, looped Eagle's reins around the rack. Doris followed suit, her boots clumping on the board sidewalk, and they went into the bank.

Like their bars and whorehouses, miners demanded service from their bank around the clock, and it would be open until nearly twilight. Its president ran suspicious eyes over Sundance, then said to Doris, "Calamity, what do you want in here? I — " He broke off as Doris pulled off the hat and her golden hair fell down around her shoulders. "Lady Bucknell!"

"That's right, Mr. Hayes. Mr. Sundance and I have some business to transact. In your private office, if you please."

Hayes blinked, but he led the way. In there, the transfer of money was soon accomplished, although Hayes seemed dubious about the whole thing. It was obvious that he could barely resist warning Doris Bucknell not to put so much money in the keeping of what was obviously a half-wild mixed blood, but he held his peace. And when Sundance, crisply and with a thorough knowledge of business procedures, arranged for the money to go to Washington, the man's manner changed. He was respectful when he ushered both of them to the front door.

Before they went out, Sundance cracked it and checked the street. He saw no sign of Drury, nothing to alarm him, but that did not mean much. "All right, Doris. Mount up, in a hurry, and I'll cover you. Head straight for the hotel and straight up to your room, I'll be right behind. We don't want to give Drury any more of a chance at you than we can help."

He liked the way she obeyed now without question, putting her trust in him. She went quickly to the horse, swung up easily, and spurred it, sending it plunging through deep mud. Sundance was already on Eagle, following, hand on his Colt, eyes shuttling from side to side. But the Deadwood House was only a few hundred yards away, a two-story frame building freshly painted, nestled against the side of the mountain. "I've got my key," Doris said, and quickly they dismounted and went in, Sundance leading, surveying the lobby as he came through the door. It was empty;

the clerk stared as they went swiftly across it and up the stairs, Sundance with drawn gun.

They reached the second floor without incident; the corridor was empty. Doris unlocked her door. "Wait," Sundance said and slammed it open so hard it banged against the wall. Gun up, he went in, but the room was empty. Doris followed him, closed the door and bolted it. Then she sighed, pulled off the hat and threw it on the bed.

"Aren't we behaving just a little foolishly?" she asked.

"Maybe," Sundance said. "But when you're dead, you're dead a long, long time. And in a deal like this, you only make one mistake. Drury could have had someone waiting for you in this room."

"I didn't even see him on the street."

"That's one reason I thought he might be here."

She took a brush from the dresser, began to pull it through her shimmering hair. "Well, what's next?"

"I'll have to spend the night with you," Sundance said, holstering the Colt.

She turned. "Will you, now?"

"No help for it. We've got to get you out of Deadwood safe and in one piece."

"You could take an adjoining room . . ."

"Too risky. They might take you and I'd never hear 'em. No. I'll sleep on the floor. Don't worry, I'll mind my manners."

She shrugged. "As you please. I suppose it is a little ridiculous to be worrying over appearances when a man has threatened my life. But right now, you're going to have to be the thorough gentleman and turn your back. These clothes of Jane's have seen better days. They smell as if her horse had been wearing them. I'm looking forward to getting out of them."

"Go ahead," Sundance said, and he faced the door.

Behind him, he heard the rustle of

clothes, first of the harsh fabric of Jane's garments, then the silky noise of finer cloth. As Doris changed, she talked, a little swiftly and jerkily, as if in response to the relief from tension.

"I suppose you're wondering why I'm not wearing mourning with my husband dead so soon. But, of course, I didn't bring any, and there's nothing much in the way of women's clothes to be had here in Deadwood. Anyhow, buying the Nez Perce horses is my way of mourning . . . " She paused. "Poor John. Twenty years in the Indian Army and never a scratch; he comes to America and is dead within a month."

"Twenty years," Sundance said in surprise. "He must have been considerably older than you."

"He was. He never married until he returned from India; that was three years ago. He was in my father's regiment, and my father arranged the match."

"A marriage of convenience?"

"Perhaps you could call it that. But

he was a good, kind man and I . . . have much affection for him. I certainly would not let his death go unavenged. For a while, Mr. Sundance, I even had the idea that perhaps I would buy a pistol and seek out Luke Drury myself. But then I thought that this would hurt Drury much worse. There . . . Now you can turn around."

Sundance did. She wore a dress of green watered silk, and she was a sight to take away a man's breath. It hugged her bosom, outlining the round, separate mounds, clung to her slender waist, traced the fullness of her hips before the skirt obscured them.

She read the reaction her appearance produced, and a faint smile touched her lips. Then she sobered. "What shall we do about the horses?"

"When Jane comes, I'll have her put them in the livery. She ought to be here almost any minute, if she didn't go to sleep up on the mountain, sucking on that bottle."

"She's quite a character. Is it true

that she was the only woman the famous Wild Bill Hickok really loved?"

Sundance laughed. "No, but she likes to think it is. I — " He broke off as there was a hammering at the door, and Doris gasped as his gun was suddenly in his hand. He shoved her aside, so that no slug coming through the thin panel would catch her, eased clear of the line of fire himself. "Who is it?"

"Only me, Sundance," Jane Canary's voice said, a little thickly.

Sundance eased. She sounded as if she'd killed the bottle, but she could hold a lot of booze and still function, and she'd be useful tonight and tomorrow morning. He went to the door, pouching the Colt. "Okay, Jane," He slid the bolt, turned the key, and opened the door.

Then he froze.

"Don't move, Sundance," Luke Drury said. His nose was bandaged, his face covered with tape. He stood behind Jane Canary with one arm locked around her throat. In his other hand, he held a gun, its muzzle centered on Sundance's belly. So were the bores of the Colts of the four men who stood there with him, and under the dead drop of five guns, Sundance knew they had him.

"Jim," Jane Canary husked. "I didn't go to — They caught me comin' in the hotel and laid their guns on me and made me — "

"It's all right," said Sundance. Slowly he raised his hands.

Drury said, "Chet. Git his gun and that damn Bowie knife."

"Right." A lanky, bearded man moved forward. He was, Sundance saw, a professional, never blocking the line of fire of his mates. He pulled the gunbelt loose, let it drop with its burden of Colt and Bowie, and kicked it across the room.

"Awright, Luke. He's slick."

"Good. Now, one of you take Calamity into that room across the hall. Jane, you like booze so much, you're gonna git your fill. We got a whole bottle of it for you, and you ain't leavin' this hotel until you've drunk it, and more if that's what it takes to knock you out. Me, I'd rather use a pistol barrel, but you're too popular around here. So you git off light. Sundance, here, he don't have it so easy."

One of the men pulled Jane away. Drury stepped forward then, cut, puffed lips pulling back from his teeth in a kind of snarl. The others followed him, guns unwavering. One closed the door.

"Now, lady," Drury said. "If you're smart, you won't make a noise. That way, you git to live a while longer." His eyes met Sundance's; one of them was nearly shut. They gleamed with hatred. "And you, you God damned half breed," Drury rasped, "I still owe you a gunwhippin' "

Sundance went tense, but he had no chance to move as, suddenly, Drury's gun came up and its long barrel lashed sideways. It slammed against his head, and the last thing he heard was Doris's frightened gasp. Then the world exploded in a flare of brightness and after that there was total darkness.

At first, there was only pain. It seemed as if an iron rod ran clear through his skull, in one temple, out the other, and it was as if someone were pulling on it, trying to pry the top of his head off. The pain sickened him and made him retch, and he heard from far away a voice. "Luke, I think he's wakin' up."

"Good," said Drury's voice. "Throw some water on the bastard and make it faster. I've waited long enough."

Sundance lay motionless. With an effort of will, he gathered up the tattered ends of faculties and senses, forced his mind to work. He lay on a floor of hard-packed dirt, and there was, in the room, the smell of burning wood and coal oil. That meant a fireplace and lamps; added to the floor, he knew he was in a cabin. Drury was here and several other men and — tentatively, he moved his hands and found them bound behind his back.

Then a cascade of icy water sluiced over him. It nearly strangled him, but it jerked him back to full consciousness and his eyes came open. He looked into the face of one of Drury's men, who, grinning, sloshed the rest of the bucket on him. "Okay, Luke," the man said. "He's all yourn."

It was a cabin, all right, one room of unpeeled logs; and it was night; Sundance could see moonlight through the gaps in mud chinking. Stiffly, he sat up; it cost him another wave of sickening pain, but when that faded to a dull throb he was fairly sure it would not come again.

Drury was coming to him, in the firelight, battered lips grinning without mirth, nose still encased in bandage wrappings. His four gunmen were ranged around the walls. Then Sundance stiffened. Doris Bucknell was slumped in one corner, face smudged, hair awry, the green dress ripped to tatters around her breasts. She looked at Sundance with dull hopelessness, and Sundance guessed immediately the ordeal she had endured. He fought back the white, knife-edged anger that sprang up in him, knowing he would need all his coolness and clarity if he were to survive at all.

"Well," Drury said thickly, towering above him. "The great Jim Sundance wasn't so hard to take after all. Eh?" His mouth twisted and his boot lashed out, and pain flared in Sundance's flank as the toe smashed against his ribs. He fell back, gasping.

"Now," Drury said, thumbs hooked in gunbelt. "We got some things to settle, Sundance. I got one Appaloosa stallion now, yeah, that horse of yours. But there's six more and a bunch of mares I got to git my hands on. You're gonna take us to those horses. Every time you raise a fuss, you're gonna git the livin' hell beat out of you. And, wherever they are, if they ain't there when we git there, you're gonna

96

die awful slow and awful hard. With that in mind, Sundance, suppose you tell me where they are and how long a trip we got to rig out for."

Sundance knew nothing but to play for time. His philosophy was this: when you were dead, all chances were ended. As long as you remained alive, there was, down to the last crucial second, some chance anyway. He shook his head as if thoroughly dazed, which was not far from the truth. "It's . . . long," he said thickly.

"Damn you, I figured that!" Drury kicked him again. "Now, git down to cases! Where? Here in the Black Hills? Is that why you had Bucknell come to Deadwood?"

"No. No, they're a long way from here."

Drury let out a breath. "That would mean west and likely north. The Bearpaws, the Bitterroots, the Absorokas, Montana, Idaho, Washin'ton, Or'gon — Where, damn it? Answer me?"

97

Sundance said, "For God's sake, Drury. I can't think. My head hurts. You've near kicked in my ribs. I got to have some water."

"Awright, Leroy," Drury said after a moment. "Bring the dipper."

"Jim," Doris Bucknell said thickly from across the little room. "Jim, don't tell them, do you hear? Those horses are mine, now!"

Drury whirled on her. "Shut up, you damned Limey bitch! Or — " He grinned savagely. "You want some more of what you already had?"

Doris raised her head and looked at him. "I'm not afraid of you, Drury. I was taught to have nothing but contempt for scum."

"Scum?" Drury roared the word, clenched big fists, took a step toward her. "I'll have you lickin' my damn boots before I'm through with you!"

"Doris," Sundance said, and he meant it. "Be quiet. Drury's right. He's got us cold." He drank water from the dipper, felt a certain amount of strength return. As Leroy straightened up, he said, "All right, Drury. I'll deal with you."

"Deal?" Drury spun toward him. "Deal, hell. You'll tell me what I want to know. That's all there is to it. You'll take me to the horses!"

"Only," Sundance said, "if you let Lady Bucknell go."

"*Lady* Bucknell." Drury stared at him, and one corner of his battered mouth curled up. "She ain't no lady, now, Sundance. Not after — "

"I said, you let her go, I'll take you to the horses."

Drury snorted. "No chance. You think I'd turn her loose to run to some British consul and raise a stink? Uh-uh. She goes with us out of town, dressed like a man, the way she come in a while ago. Maybe we'll haul her along for two days, three, maybe for a week or so, if she's real nice to me and the rest of us. But sooner or later . . . " He made a gesture. "I can't afford to have her found dead

99

here, not after her husband was already rubbed out, that would make too much of a stink. But if she just disappears, then nobody can prove nothin'. She went off with that half-breed, eh? If they ever find her bones, they'll figure that halfbreed killed her. That's how it stacks up, Sundance. Now . . . you talk, with no more waste of breath. If you don't, you git hurt. And you can holler all you want, because this ole cabin's a long way down the gulch. Ain't nothin' around us but a few Goddamn Chinamen, and they don't see, hear, nor speak nothin'. Not when it's white man's business."

And that, Sundance knew, was true. No help could be expected from that quarter, even if they were heard.

"Now," said Drury. "Let's have an end to all this yammer. Where did you take the horses, Sundance, when you left the Bearpaws?"

Sundance drew in a long breath that made his battered ribs ache. "All right," he said. "They're in the Bitterroots."

Drury blinked. "The Bitterroots? Hell's fire, that's clean across Montana from here! Where in the Bitterroots?"

"No way I could tell you," Sundance said. "I'll have to take you there. I could draw you a map and you'd still never find it."

Drury looked at him a moment, chewing his lip. Then he nodded. "That figures. You goddamn Injuns still know a lot of secret places. You wouldn't have put those horses in any place a white man could find." Suddenly his boot lashed out again, smashing against Sundance's ribs with terrible force. Sundance grunted and fell back.

"Okay," Drury said. "We'll line out first thing in the mornin'. That means I got a lot to do tonight. Got to git together horses and an outfit, have that big Appaloosa of yours sent west to my ranch — I don't aim to lose him, he's worth a fortune in stud fees — and . . ." He turned. "Leroy, you and Chet stay here and watch these two. Take turns, I want somebody awake the whole damned time. This halfbreed's as slippery as calf slobber and as dangerous as a rattlesnake. Fred and Mart'll come with me. We'll be back at first daylight with an outfit and ready to haul tail outa here."

Leroy said, "Boss, what about Calamity Jane? She's got an awful big mouth."

Drury laughed. "She's got more'n a quart of whiskey in her, too, and I left twenty dollars in her pocket. She'll wake up tomorrow mornin' so damned addled she won't know what happened and she'll take that twenty and head for a bar to clear her head. By the time she starts to spout about what happened, nobody will pay her no nevermind. It'll be like that tall story of hers about bein' Wild Bill Hickok's woman." He shrugged. "It would be easier to kill her, yeah, but she's kinda a town pet. That *would* make some stink. No, she's a drunk whore and everybody knows it and nobody believes nothin' that a drunk whore says. Don't worry about her. You just keep your eyes on Sundance and this English bitch. You hear?"

Leroy nodded. "We'll do that."

"You better, for the premium wages I'm layin' out. Come on, you fellers." Drury went to the door, and there he paused. "Sundance." He touched his bandaged nose. "You hurt me bad today. But that's all right. I aim to hurt you just as bad from time to time. You'll live to rue the day you ever whipped Luke Drury." Then, followed by two gunmen, he went out.

After the door had closed behind him, the man called Leroy came to stand over Jim Sundance. He drew his gun and aimed it at the half breed's head. He was slat-thin, with a hard, pockmarked face and an enormous Adams-apple in his scrawny neck. "Roll over, half breed," he said.

Sundance did so, aided by Leroy's rough boot in his painful flank. With his face against the dirt floor, he lay still

103

while Leroy checked the ropes around his wrist and his ankles, which were also bound. Like Chet, the man was a professional, and when he was through, there was no slack left at all in the bonds. They were, Sundance realized, of hemp, which, unlike rawhide, did not stretch with changes in the moisture content of the air. That was bad; but, as if reading Sundance's mind, Leroy said: "I learned a long time ago never to tie a man up with rawhide, not in a damp place like this. You know how I learned that, Sundance?"

When Sundance didn't answer, he went on.

"The hard way, Injun. I used to scout for wagon trains. One day a bunch of Blackfeet caught me cold, while I was waterin' my horse. I thought they'd kill me right off, but they didn't. You know what they did? They tied me up against a tree so I couldn't move, layin' on my side. Then they caught a rattlesnake and tied that with a rawhide thong, too, right in front of my face.

They rode off and left me with that snake tied up just short enough so he couldn't hit me when he struck. But they knowed about rawhide, and that when evenin' dew come on that snake's thong would stretch. They figured that come mornin' he'd have slack enough to hit me right between the eyes. That was a long night, Sundance. That snake come at me again and again, closer every time. It was pure damn luck that some people from the wagon train found me before that piggin' string stretched another eighth of an inch, or I'd be rottin' in the ground right now." He straightened up. "I tell you this for two reasons. One, to let you know you don't have a prayer of gittin' out of those ropes. The other is to make damn sure you know how bad I hate Injuns and why. I aim to watch you, I aim to watch you hard and all the time, and if you move bad at all, I'll hurt you so much you can't stand it. Right?"

Sundance didn't answer. He rolled

over on his back, and, hurting from the punishment he had taken, watched the firelight play on the rafters and shingled roof overhead. Leroy said, "Chet, you go ahead and catch some shut-eye. I'll watch this halfbreed bastard and the Limey slut."

Chet, bearded, lanky, yawned and stretched. "Fair enough." He went to a rickety bunk in one corner, threw himself down on its hard boards. Presently his rhythmic snoring was audible in the room.

Leroy sat there with gun in hand, watching Sundance. "Break," he said quietly. "Just break. Oh, God, I hope you try to. I'll hurt you so bad . . ."

*Break*, Sundance thought bitterly. There was no chance of that. Not the way he was bound and watched. His fear was not for himself; he knew that he still had days and weeks to live. But Doris Bucknell — Obviously, they had already brutalized her, violated her, and as soon as they were clear of Deadwood, in a place where her body never would be found . . .

An hour passed as he lay on the dirt floor and Leroy never slackened his watchful guard. It was one of the longest ones Jim Sundance had ever lived through. Memories surged unbidden through his mind: the old Cheyenne rulership of the high prairies, his parents lying dead on the buffalo grass north of Bent's Fort, one of the Pawnees finally screaming when he avenged their murder: and other, more recent ones. He remembered Little Big Horn and Custer's startled face as Jim Sundance's bullet struck home, destroying the man who had killed the Cheyennes on the Washita, who had opened the Black Hills of the Sioux to settlement to enlarge his own image, who had been the worst enemy the Indians ever had . . . And Crook. He remembered George Crook, too, the only General of the Army who, as it turned out, an Indian could trust. Crook had been like a father to Jim Sundance and had told him how politics worked in Washington. Crook had found the lawyer for him and had worked in the Indians' behalf. Crook was far away now, and isolated; there was not much room in the Army now for a General who liked Indians.

So much had changed so fast in so few years. When Sundance's father, who had borne another name, had come west from England, the black sheep of his family, paid to stay away, the Indians had trusted white men. Sundance's father had loved their clean, hard, honorable way of life. When, the first white man allowed to do that, he had participated in the most sacred ceremony of the plains tribes, the Sun Dance, he had given up his own name and taken Sundance instead. Jim Sundance had also participated in the ceremony. Now there were scars on his chest where the skin had been slit to run ropes through. At the end of those ropes had trailed heavy buffalo skulls, and the young Jim Sundance had danced and danced until the weight of them ripped his flesh and the ropes fell loose. After that, he had been initiated into the Dog Soldiers . . .

Less than twenty years, he thought bitterly. And so much of what he had attempted had ended in failure. And now . . .

He tensed.

For a moment, he thought that he had lost his senses. Maybe he had been hurt too much. He lay very still.

Under his back, it happened again. The ground seemed to move, the hardpacked dirt floor of the cabin vibrating silently. He focused all his faculties; and then he understood. Not completely, but this much: that there was a hollow or an opening of some sort under where he lay and somebody was in it, a tunnel like a mine shaft. And whoever was there was working steadily to come up beneath him, but in utter silence.

Sundance lay rigid. Under his body, the floor seemed to shift and work; yet, there was no sound. He looked at Leroy. The man was watching him with malevolent intensity, only hoping that he would dare to break.

Jim Sundance turned his head. Slumping against her bonds in the corner, Doris Bucknell had fallen into fitful sleep.

Sundance said, "Leroy."

"Yeah." The man leaned forward eagerly, gun lined.

"Her. The English woman. How was it?"

Under his back, there was more subterranean activity. He had no idea what it meant, but it must mean something, and Leroy's attention had to be diverted.

"How was it?" Leroy said. He grinned. "Sundance, you ought to know."

"I don't." Sundance grinned lewdly. "You came in too early."

"Well, I'll tell you how it was," Leroy said. He turned, looked toward the girl. Beneath Sundance something fell away. He felt cool air on his bound wrists. "It was too damned quick, that's how it was." He looked at the slumbering girl. "Of course, right now I got her all to myself."

"Leroy," Sundance said, "you'd be a swine to — "

"Yeah. It would bother you, wouldn't it?" Leroy stared at the woman, then arose and went to her. "You'd have to lay there and watch . . . "

Sundance only knew this: that there was a hole now under his body. A gap in the dirt floor. Cool air, as if from a tunnel, blew on his wrists. Then somebody touched a bound hand reassuringly, and in caution. He did not move.

"Yeah, you could watch," Leroy said. He cupped Doris Bucknell's chin, raised her head, and she came awake with a start, looking at him with fear.

"But first," Leroy said, "I'll wake up Chet. Because you got to be watched, Sundance. You got to be watched every minute." He walked across the cabin, bent over the bunk. "Hey, Chet. I got an idea — "

The hand stroked Sundance's through the opening beneath his body. Then he felt the knifeblade begin to cut his ropes. One by one, they parted.

"Chet, damn it," Leroy said.

Sundance lay like a block of wood. The ropes around his wrists fell away. He flexed his hands.

"Chet, wake up — "

Blood stung, as circulation returned. Then Sundance sucked in a breath.

His hands were pulled down through the hole in the floor under his body. Something was crammed into the right one; the butt of a Colt revolver. Sundance's fingers curled around grip, trigger, hammer.

"Chet — " Leroy shook the man roughly. Chet rolled over, grunted.

"Damn it," he said.

Sundance did not dare come up yet. He had to have better circulation in his hands. He flexed fingers, twisted wrists. Chet sat up. "What is it, Leroy?"

"Your turn to take watch. I got some business with this woman."

Doris Bucknell, awake now, sucked in a breath of terror. "Please," she said, voice trembling, touseled hair hanging over her face.

"You beg, lady," Leroy said. "It pleasures me to hear you beg. Chet, watch that half breed. I intend to make her beg some more." He turned away from the bunk, went to Doris Bucknell, as Chet, blinking, sat up. "Lady," he said, hooking his hand in her tattered bodice. "Lady, this time you're all mine." He turned his back to Sundance, staring down at Doris' breasts. Chet rolled off the bunk.

Sundance came up with the gun. He swung on Chet first. He felt the Colt jump in his hand as he pulled the trigger. Chet looked totally astonished and fell back, as a bullet ploughed through his heart. Leroy whirled, eyes widening, hand flashing down to holster.

Sundance fired twice more. The first

bullet caught Leroy in the belly and knocked him back against the wall. Leroy screamed. The second blew his head apart, and the scream ended instantaneously. His mutilated body slumped to the floor.

The room was rank with powder-smoke. Doris Bucknell made a strangled sound in her throat. Sundance rolled, came up again, and now the floor where he had lain seemed to have caved in. There was a big hole there, and in it a saffron, pigtailed head popped up. Then a lean body in loose pajamas boiled out, and two more came behind, with hatchets in hand, poised.

The three Chinese dragged Sundance to his feet. A hatchet's blade severed the ropes around his ankles. Sundance stared as the men ran to Doris Bucknell, chopped her bonds. One Chinese lifted her to her feet, dragged her across the room. Another pointed to the gaping hole in the dirt floor. "Down," he said.

114

Sundance slid through the hole, keeping the gun ready. He landed in a dark tunnel, lit only by a coal oil lamp held by another Chinaman crouching there. Behind him, Doris Bucknell landed lithely. The Chinese with the lamp said, "Come," and gestured.

When he turned, Sundance saw a long, low, timbered tunnel, not unlike a mine shaft, stretching away before him. He took Doris Bucknell's arm and they ran behind the Chinaman. For a little while, Sundance had his bearings. Then he lost them completely. The tunnel ran and swooped and curved and doubled, and other tunnels intersected it, and all Sundance could do was follow the light.

Beside him, at a turn, Doris stumbled, brought up panting. Tunnels, like the working of a gopher's home or a prairie dog town, went in every direction. "Jim," she gasped. "I — "

"I don't understand either. All I know is that we've got to go." He clasped the Colt tightly, helped her to follow the Chinese with the lamp.

Another hundred yards straight down a shaft; then, suddenly, there was space and light. They emerged into a timbered, underground room, ten yards across, thirty long. On one flank was an altar, and on it were wicker baskets filled with human bones. The air was heavy with the smell of incense and a sweeter smell: Sundance recognized it: Opium.

In the centre of the room, there was a low table, and woven reed mats around it. The man with the lamp blew out his light as he went to it, for torches on the wall shed illumination enough. Then, from behind the table, another figure reared itself, and a voice said, in perfect English, "Welcome, Mr. Sundance. Our poor house is yours."

Jim Sundance stood stiffly, looking at the man, while Doris leaned wearily against him. "You," said Sundance.

In the rich robes he wore, red with gold and black embroidery, the

Chinese whom Sundance had saved from the bullwhacker that morning no longer looked small and wispy. He was imposing, almost majestic. "Yes," he said. "It is I. I had not expected to be able to repay the favor so soon." He gestured to the mats before the table. "Please sit down. I know you are very tired and have been through much. Here, believe me, you are completely safe. The whole force of the On Leong guarantees that."

"The On Leong."

"You are familiar with it?"

"It's a tong," Sundance said. "A Chinese fighting society."

"Yes." The old man smiled. "Like your Cheyenne Dog Soldiers. Now, please. There will be hot tea and food and whiskey if you want it."

"I want it," Sundance said, sinking to a mat, Doris dropping beside him and leaning against him. The old man clapped his hands. From each wall, where they had been concealed in niches, other Chinese appeared. The old man said something in a high, musical dialect. Two bowed, burly, and, Sundance noted, carrying hatchets in loops at their waists. They went out. The others squatted. The old man sank behind the table and leaned his elbows on it, folding his hands together.

"My name is Tsu Chao," he said. "It would be easier if you called me Mr. Tsu. I know you have many questions. Of course, you understand that there are many people from the Celestial Empire in Deadwood."

"Yes," Sundance said. "A lot of Chinamen."

"Indeed." Mr. Tsu stroked his gray chinwhiskers. "Thousands of my countrymen have been brought in to build your railroads and work your mines. Many of them came to the Black Hills when gold was discovered. Unfortunately, problems of language and custom have separated us from the Americans. We have built

118

our own town here on lower Main Street. Even so, we had no peace. The white men seem to hate everyone with skin of a different color, as I think you have good reason to know. So we went underground. When we built our temples above ground, they were desecrated and destroyed. When those of us who have the opium habit indulged, they were arrested. The Chinese have been abused and wronged everywhere in Deadwood. So, we constructed a city of our own beneath the town."

He gestured. "These tunnels run up and down the gulch. There are entries and exits here and there in unexpected places, so, if there were mass persecution of our people, there would always be a place to hide. We have our joss houses, temples, and our whole civilization here. Above ground, we are despised common laborers; below it, we are ourselves."

A burly Chinese came with tea and whiskey. Sundance poured a shot of the whiskey into a cup of tea, handed it to Doris, and she drank it greedily. He took a drink straight from the bottle, then picked up a cup of tea to sip it. Strong, it refreshed him marvelously.

Mr. Tsu himself sipped a cup of tea. "Up there," he pointed, "they call me Uncle Billygoat." He stroked his gray chin whiskers. "Up there I am only what they call a swamper in the Deadwood House, the hotel. Down here, however, I am a man of power. You understand, Sundance, that we must look after our own. The two societies, rivals, to be sure, the Hip Sings and the On Leongs, have, nevertheless, joined forces in Deadwood to protect our people, and I am leader of the combined tongs. Perhaps that is because I speak the best English of any Chinese in Deadwood, though they shall never know that up above. Be that as it may, when you helped me out of difficulty this morning, I marked you well. We always repay our obligations, you know. Then tonight, there was trouble — but who would pay attention to old Uncle Billy goat, emptying the spittoons and garbage?"

He smiled. "We have a good information-gathering network. I know about you, about Drury, about the horses. None of that concerns me, except that I have a debt, my very life, to repay. So . . . they took you from the hotel to a cabin on lower Main. They had no idea that we had an entrance through the floor of that deserted cabin, which was abandoned long ago. Boards, and then the dirt laid over it. It was not difficult to come to you from beneath and give you the gun you used so expertly. Now the boards are replaced, the floor brushed down, no trace of your exit there. Here, for so long as you want to stay, you are completely safe."

Sundance was silent for a moment, absorbing all this. When he had it locked in his mind, he nodded. "Now I am in your debt, Mr. Tsu."

"Not at all. We are only even."

"All the same," Sundance said, "we've got to get out of here."

"No one will ever find you."

"That doesn't matter. I have things to do."

"Ah, yes," said Mr. Tsu. "The horses. The Indian horses."

"That's right," Sundance said.

Mr. Tsu folded his hands. "Then tell me what you require."

Sundance reached for the bottle, took his second drink of whiskey. He thought about Drury and red rage rose within him, but Drury could wait. The main thing was to get the horses and drive them to the railroad. "I need my Appaloosa stallion," he said, "and I need a good horse for Lady Bucknell. I need the gear on my horse, the two big saddlebags. I need my rifle, and I think we ought to have an extra one for Lady Bucknell, and some extra blankets. I need ammunition for a Colt and a Winchester, both .44 caliber. Is all that too much to ask?"

Mr. Tsu smiled. "I think it is very little. You shall have it. There is only one problem. That is your stallion. We have seen how he has fought everyone who came near him. He is in the livery and it will be hard for strangers, men with our distinctive smell at that, to take him out. How shall we manage that?"

Sundance pulled off his hat, shrugged off his buckskin shirt. The torso thus revealed was coppery, rippling with muscle, scarred with old wounds. "Put this shirt over his head. He'll go anywhere with you then. Mr. Tsu, we want to be out of Deadwood and on our way before first light. Can you manage that?"

"I think it will be no problem," Mr. Tsu said. "We would kill Drury for you if we could, but we understand that he had connections with your Army. That makes it very risky for us."

Sundance said, "Leave Drury to me. Only get me an outfit together."

Mr. Tsu shoved the bottle toward

him. "Never fear, Mr. Sundance," he said. "It shall be done." Then he gestured towards a darkened tunnel entrance. "But now, I think you and the lady must rest."

# 5

ALL around them, land and sky seemed endless. They had come down out of the Black Hills and were now working their way northwest across the limitless prairie of eastern Montana. As a hump of ground loomed before them, absolutely treeless, furred only with dun grass, Sundance reined in Eagle.

"You go down there in the draw and wait for me. I'll scout ahead."

"Yes." Doris Bucknell had learned to obey his commands implicitly. As he dropped off of Eagle, she gathered the Appaloosa's reins and loped her own good horse down into concealment. Sundance, rifle in hand, went up the hill on foot, running low, crouched, and before he reached the crest, flinging himself on his belly, peering around, not over, a tuft of grass.

Before him, the land stretched endlessly, emptily. Once Cheyennes, Blackfeet, Piegans, a few stray Flatheads and Nez Perce, and Crows from the south had ranged across these hunting grounds above the Yellowstone. Now the Indians were gone, only a few hundred white men were left to fill the hugely vacant land. Since there was no gold out here, and they had not yet come with cattle, Sundance did not expect to see anyone, and he was right. Satisfied that the way was clear, he ran back down the slope with a wolf's easy, loose-jointed gait, and joined Doris Bucknell in the draw.

"It's all right," he said. "We'll camp here."

"Good," she said, rubbing her sunburnt face with relief.

Sundance looked at her. A week had passed since Drury had taken them in Deadwood and they had fought free. But she was still in shock, too much had happened to her too fast. As he helped her make the camp, showing her

126

again how to build a nearly smokeless fire of dried sage and buffalo chips, he let his mind run back over the events of those seven days.

In the alcove of the tunnels, she had slept like someone dead in his arms. Long before dawn, Mr. Tsu had awakened them. "Your horses are here and everything that you wanted. I think it would be well if you left now."

"Yes." Sundance had followed him down a long tunnel, and with Doris had climbed a ladder that brought them out through a trapdoor in the forest south of town. There, two hulking Chinese held the horses, and they were, as Sundance found when, meticulously, he checked, loaded with everything he needed. When he had boosted Doris into the saddle and swung up himself, he had gathered her horse's reins and, striking Eagle with his heels, had wasted no time. Climbing a ridge, he had halted once, turned; below, he saw in torchlight glare in the forest Mr. Tsu. Sundance raised his hand, the Chinese did likewise, and then Sundance rode on with Doris following.

He had wintered here with the Sioux many times and knew the Black Hills like the back of his hand, and he went down hidden creeks and across barren ridges, exercising all the arts he had learned from every Indian tribe, and he had an idea that Drury, unless he also had an Indian tracker and that one a genius, could not pick up the trail. It was not Drury he worried about now. It was the United States Army. After all, the Army was behind Drury, and it sent the tentacles of its patrols out everywhere, in every unexpected direction. It had begun to build a ring of forts to hem in what had been northern high plains Indian territory, and Sundance knew that Drury must have been in touch with Sheridan in Chicago, and Sheridan must have telegraphed or sent by riders messages to all his fort in the West. *Look out for Jim Sundance . . .*

The Army had Crow scouts, and

the Crows were good fighting men. It had recruited Cheyennes, too, and also some Sioux; with the tribes starving, you could buy anybody if your price was high enough. So it was not anybody if your price was high enough. So it was not just Indian against soldier; it was Indian against Indian. Sundance was certain in his own mind that Drury would have mobilized all the forces of the Western Army under Miles and Howard against him.

That was why he traveled like a hunted animal, always masking his trail, always checking the land over the next ridge before he moved on.

Now, in the draw, he put a loin of antelope killed this morning with his bow on to cook and looked across the fire at her. Her green dress was tattered, revealing legs and bosom; the rough jacket of antelope hide he had made for her did not cover her much. Her hair was touseled, tangled, and most of it tied in a pigtail behind her neck. All the same, she bore up well.

Sundance, looking at her, knowing that here there was comparative security, for the first time in a week allowed himself to feel a natural response. She was a woman, and he had been without a woman for a long time. All the same, he was, he told himself, no Drury. She was as safe with him as she wanted to be.

They ripped into the antelope loin almost savagely, and Doris' cheeks were smeared with grease. Swallowing, washing down the meat with water from a canteen, she said, "You still haven't told me, really, where we're going. To the Bitterroots?"

"No. I lied to Drury, of course. That's not where they are."

"Then where?"

Sundance did not answer.

Doris sat up straight. "Jim!" There was anger in her voice. "Don't you think we've been together now long enough for you to trust me? I've paid twenty thousand dollars and . . . and if anything happened to you, I'd be left high and dry! Aren't I entitled to something?"

"I'm sorry," Sundance said. "But even if I told you, you couldn't find them without me. And if by some chance Drury should take us — "

"I see," she muttered bitterly. "You think he might . . . torture the information out of me. So I'm not to have it, despite the money I've paid."

"Look," Sundance said. "Those horses are all Joseph and his people have. If I can get 'em out safely, well and good. If it turns out I can't, then they can stay where they are indefinitely. There're two warriors with them, and eventually they'll come out and let Joseph know where they are and then maybe he can still sell them. But I'm not going to take the least chance of Drury or the Army getting them now. Anyhow — " his voice was hard " — if we don't get 'em out, the chances are that neither of us will be in shape for twenty thousand to mean anything to either of us, one way or the other. We'll be dead."

Her mouth thinned. "All right, so I'm to be kept in ignorance. You're a stubborn man, Jim Sundance."

He shrugged. She had a right to be angry with him, but his first duty was to the Nez Perce, and there was no help for it. "I'll tell you this much," he said. "We're not headed for the horses now. We're bound for Canada."

"Canada?"

"That's right. To Sitting Bull and his Hunkpapa Sioux. After Little Big Horn they went there, under the Queen's protection, and now they're about the last free Indians left north of Apache country. The horses are in such a place that I'll need help to get them out and to the railroad, three men and a woman can't do it alone, not and defend 'em against Drury or the Army, too. Joseph was heading to join up with Sitting Bull when the Army caught him, and a lot of Nez Perce did make it. I'm gonna ask them for help. With fifteen or twenty fighting men, I know I can get the horses out and to the railroad, and when I do that, then I'll give you title, and not even the Army will dare interfere with the property of a British subject."

His voice softened. "I know it sounds like I don't trust you. But that's not true. It's just that things have to be a certain way and — "

After a long moment, Doris nodded, and the anger left her face. "Yes. Yes, I understand. All right, I won't ask about the horses again. I'll just follow where you lead and try to help and not to hinder."

"Thanks," Sundance said, meaning it.

She turned her face away. Presently, almost as if to herself, she said, "I don't think I ever met anyone like you in my whole life. I suppose, in a way, you're like a patriot fighting for his country. Only your country is this — " She swept out an arm to encompass the whole vast lonely territory. "And its citizens are the Indians." Then she said, still not looking at him, something that startled him. "Jim. My period of mourning for John is over. He always told me that if he died, I must not mourn too long." She did look at him now, and he tensed, recognizing what he saw in her eye. "He always said that I must go on living. And . . . Jim. We have a long way to go together."

"Yes," Sundance said. "We do." He stood up, and as she shrugged out of the antelope hide jacket and reached for the fastenings of the tattered dress, he exulted in the chance to forget Drury and everything else for the moment, and, quickly, knowing what she wanted, wanting it, too, he went to her.

Riding north, they crossed the Yellowstone, the Missouri, and followed the valley of the Milk. Sundance moved now with even greater caution; patrols were always out along the border, lest Sitting Bull go to war again and swoop down unexpectedly. Three times, from a distance, they saw blueclad troops moving like ants across the enormous land, but Sundance saw to it that the soldiers never caught a glimpse of them. But, he thought, it would not be this easy coming back with ten or twenty men, and even harder when the horses were out of their hiding place and in the open. Meanwhile, of Drury there was no sign.

Then there came a day, nearly four weeks out of Deadwood, when Sundance touched Eagle with his heels and the stallion broke into a dead run, with Doris, surprised, lashing her mount to keep up. But the stallion only raced for a few hundred yards; then Sundance pulled it up, danced it around. As Doris came alongside, he pointed. The granite marker and the cairn of stones around it was almost hidden in tall grass, but they were north of it. "Now," he said with triumph in his voice. "That's the boundary, we're out of the United States and in Canada. We may have to worry about Drury, but at least the Army's off our necks, and

135

here you're a citizen. All we've got to worry about is the Northwest Mounted Police, and there're nowhere near as many of them as there are American soldiers."

Doris sighed with relief. "Thank God, it's almost like being home. But why should we have to worry about the Canadian Mounties?"

"Because," Sundance said, "they're not going to take kindly to anybody leading twenty or so Indians still classified as hostiles back into the U.S. So we're better off dodging 'em if we can." He swung the stallion. "Now, on to Sitting Bull. We've still got nearly five hundred miles to go."

As they pointed north again, Sundance thought that it was no wonder that the Hunkpapa Sioux had fled to this place and remained. This country was as Montana had been until five years ago. Buffalo still grazed on endless rolling prairie, moose and elk were shadowy in the big forests. Once they saw a grizzly on its hind legs, watching them with unfearing curiosity, like some huge, shaggy idol.

Nine days over the border, Sundance began to see signs of former camps, circles of campfire stones, the dragmarks of travois, abandoned meat-drying racks. Increasingly, these signs were fresher. There were a lot of Indians up here in Canada right now, most of them Sitting Bull's *Hunkpapa oyati*, but Minneconjou, Sans Arc, and Black Moccasin Sioux as well. Sundance had no need to look for them; he knew they would find him first.

They did. Crossing the divide between two creeks, they traveled through the dimness of a spruce forest. Horses had been along this trail not long before. Presently, without knowing how, Sundance became aware that they were being watched. There was not a sound, nothing more than the constant mourning of breeze in treetops, but they were there, in the woods. He rode on with his hands high, well away from his guns.

Then, with no warning, they appeared. Like drifting fog, five of them, on horseback, materialized in the trail ahead; more were on the flanks and others in the rear; they were encircled, and a gasp broke from Doris.

"It's all right," Sundance said. "Stand fast." He raised one hand, addressing the leader of the Indians who barred the trail. "*Haukolah*, Hawk Circling. I haven't seen you since the Greasy Grass."

"Sundance." The man trotted his spotted pony forward. He was in his thirties, muscular, and he had fought well at Little Big Horn. He carried a rifle cradled in his arms, and he leaned out of the saddle to take Sundance's hand.

After the greetings were over, Hawk Circling, too polite to inquire about the woman, said, "So you finally tired of the old place. You have come here to be free again."

"I have come to see Sitting Bull and Yellow Wolf of the Nez Perce. He's with you, isn't he?"

"Yes. We've many Nez Perce with us. In the old days sometimes we fought them, but now we are all one people. Come on, I'll take you to the camp." He turned his horse, and motioned with his hand. "*Hokay hey! Let's go!*"

For Sundance, it was like coming home after a long absence. There were no more Indian camps like this below the border.

Here, in the valley of a creek, a hundred lodges or more, sending pale fingers of smoke skyward, ranging up and downstream on one bank; on the other grazed a huge pony herd. Among it Sundance saw a few Appaloosas. Buffalo, deer, elk and moose meat dried in plenty on racks among the teepees, and there was the nostalgic fragrance of sweetgrass mingled with wood smoke. Doris Bucknell drew in a breath of awe.

"Take a good look," Sundance said,

as they rode through the camp, Hawk Circling going ahead to chant the news of their coming. "You may never see its like again."

When they halted in the middle of the village, men, women, children crowded in around. Many knew Sundance and called out greetings and he answered them in turn. Then they made way as a tall, brawny Indian in a Hudson's Bay blanket strode through to where Sundance sat the Appaloosa. There was excitement and a kind of hunger on his handsome face. "Sundance! It's good to see you! You have news from Thunder Rolling in the Mountains?"

Sundance shook his hand. "I have, Yellow Wolf, but it's not very good. I'm glad you're here. You're the one I want to see — you and Sitting Bull."

Yellow Wolf, *Hermene Moxmox*, of the Nez Perce, was years younger than Jim Sundance, but even so, he was the most famous breeder of horses among the Nez Perce, save for Joseph the final authority on the management of the herd. He had also been among the fiercest fighters of the tribe, and Joseph had forced him to leave to look for the women and children separated from the band and to take them to freedom. Horseman and fighting man, he was also tribal historian, and his eyes were keenly intelligent as he looked at Sundance. "Yes. We must talk about Joseph. We have many things to talk about."

Then Sitting Bull appeared, dodging through the door of one of the largest lodges, which was ornate with picture writing. The great leader of the Teton Sioux, mastermind of Little Big Horn, had aged in the past two years, Sundance noted. His hair was threaded with silver, his forehead furrowed. But he was still erect, if not tall, muscular, and his hand-shake was firm. "You have a new woman? You have not stolen her to bring the Mounties on us, or to make trouble with the Queen?"

"No," Sundance said. "She is a subject of the Queen who comes of her own free will. But she needs the help of Sitting Bull and Yellow Wolf."

"Then come into the lodge," Sitting Bull said. "And we will talk."

Doris looked around with curiosity when they entered the teepee. It was compactly arranged, with fighting gear nearly stowed, buffalo robe beds, and back rests made of rib bones and wood around the fire. A special concession was made; she was allowed to stay with Sundance and sit with the men. There was smoking, eating, and then, after the other women had withdrawn, the serious talk began. Although Sioux still occasionally raided below the boundary line, the leader of the Hunkpapa was hungry for news and so were the other chiefs who had joined them. Yellow Wolf was the most impatient of all. "Joseph," he said. "Tell me about Joseph."

Sundance did, and slowly Yellow Wolf's face grew hard. "He should have known it," he said bitterly. "He should have known that they would

142

not keep their promises. He and all the rest should have run with us or died fighting . . . Kansas. A strange land and a bad one, I have heard it from the Modocs." Then he leaned forward. "But the horses, the stallions and the mares. You have saved them?"

Sundance nodded.

Yellow Wolf's eyes lit. "Where are they?"

Slowly, Sundance shook his head. "I can't tell you that yet."

There was a moment during which all the friendship seeped out of the Nez Perce's face and it was like something carved from stone. "You can't tell me? Those are our horses, Sundance! They belong to us, to the Nez Perce! We need them now, here, in Canada!"

"They are Joseph's horses," Sundance said. "And Joseph is leader of the Nez Perce. Still. Even of you, here in Canada. He has made me promise not to tell where they are until they are safely sold and delivered . . . into this woman's hands."

Yellow Wolf stared at Doris. "Sold? To Her? To a white woman? No! Joseph can't do that with our horses! You can't!"

"There is no other way," Sundance said.

Yellow Wolf sprang to his feet. "I think there is! I think — " Instinctively his hand went to the Colt on his hip. "I — "

Then Sitting Bull was up, between them. "Wait," he said harshly. "Wait and let Sundance finish. Maybe he still has things to say."

"I have things to say, all right." Sundance's voice was rough, too. "About starving women and children and . . . Sit down, Yellow Wolf and listen!"

Yellow Wolf's nostrils flared and he drew in a long breath. But his hand came away from his knife. "All right," he said. "Then talk. I will hear you out, but I still say — " He broke off and sat down, and Sundance leaned forward and began to speak.

When he was through, Yellow Wolf still sat tensely, unreconciled. "I still do not think — "

Sitting Bull interrupted him, his deep voice gentle, but strong. "My friend."

Yellow Wolf turned to stare at the Sioux Chief. Sitting Bull's face was grave. "It is not pleasant, no. But in these days few things are. You and the other Nez Perce here could use those horses, yes. But your lives do not depend on them. Look — " He gestured. "You live still in your own way in country like your home. You still have buffalo to hunt and mountains to climb to pray on. Most important of all, you still have freedom, and the chance to make a choice, for on the day when you choose to die like a warrior, you can do it. But Joseph and the others, your friends and relatives. They have nothing left; no buffalo, no mountains, no freedom, and only one way to die, and that by hunger or disease in a strange, far country. It is our way when we have something to give it to those who have nothing; that is why we took you in when you came to us last year. You have much, now, still, and Joseph very little. It is up to you to make things equal, to give him what he needs. It is not my affair, but I know Jim Sundance; he is my godson. If he says this is true, it is true, and if he says it is right to do it thus, it is right, and if he says Joseph needs the money for the horses to feed his people, then I think the horses more important to Joseph than to you. I only know that if *I* had the horses and selling them would help my people penned up below the border like the white man's pigs, I would sell them, and at once! But it is not my affair. I have spoken." Sundance knew he would say no more on the subject. The decision was up to Yellow Wolf.

Who sat motionless, staring into the embers of the fire. Then, suddenly his shoulders slumped and he bent his head and covered his face with his hands. Sundance knew he grieved now for Joseph and for the Nez Perce horses, which he must have counted on having for his own band of free people, and which were a symbol of great importance to him. He knew, too, that he grieved for more than that, for the old days and all the people already dead, everything that had happened to the Nez Perce that could not be undone.

"Jim," Doris whispered. She was staring at Yellow Wolf strangely, having followed the conversation roughly through Sundance's oblique translation.

"Hush," Sundance told her gently.

Presently, Yellow Wolf raised his head. "Sitting Bull is right," he said, his face holding its iron composure once more. "What must be done must be done. All right, Sundance. What do you require of us?"

"Fifteen warriors," Sundance said. "To go down to the States with me and help me take the horses from where they are to the American railroad to be shipped across the water."

"And what will happen to them after that, the men? How will they get back to Canada?"

"If we can dodge the soldiers and Drury and don't have to fight," Sundance said, "I don't think it will be too hard. But — "

"Yes, but — " Yellow Wolf said, face grave. "But it's a big risk. We'll have to be prepared not to come back. Maybe prepared to die or go live in Kansas with Joseph like sheep or pigs." He stood up. "Well, that does not matter. We have decided and we'll do it. Now that you have my promise, will you tell me where the horses are and what we are to do?"

"Of course," Sundance said. "They're in the Absaroka Mountains, near where we crossed them. In what white men call Yellowstone National Park."

Doris gasped, and Yellow Wolf blinked. "Their National Park? But it swarms with white men!"

"Not where the horses are," Sundance answered, smiling. "You remember where we came down of the Lodgepole Divide? A canyon with a mouth so narrow only one horse at a time could travel? And straight up and down, so steep and rough — "

"I remember," Yellow Wolf said. "With seven hundred people, going through there was like a bad dream."

"And worse for the Army, because they didn't have Appaloosas. Anyhow, there's another canyon branching off that one, and you go in by a trail along a cliff, not much more than a mountain sheep path. I *know* the cavalry can't follow that one; we had hell's own time getting the Appaloosas over it. But we did, and they're at the bottom of the canyon in a big hole with good grass, water, and winter shelter."

He paused. "When we took the horses from the Bear Paws, I thought hard about where to hide 'em. All the northern mountains are almost wide open, miners, ranchers, the Army patrolling and mapping, timber being cut, and the Bannacks and Flatheads and a lot of other Indians still hunting there. But nobody can hunt or mine or ranch in Yellowstone Park, the Army hardly patrols it. A lot of visitors come, yeah, but only to see the boiling springs that shoot into the air, the geysers. They don't, nobody does, go back into the Absarokas, and especially not into those two canyons. How can they when only Appaloosas can make the trip?"

Grinning, he went on. "So I hid them under the white men's noses, and Two Trees and Dead Man Walking are there with them now. We know they haven't been found, or Drury wouldn't have been after us. But it won't be easy getting them out or to a railroad. Still, there's a way. One that may allow the Nez Perce to get clear and make it back to Canada."

"And that is?"

"We go back along our old trail through the Absarokas, west. Then we swing west and south, hiding in the mountains, down to Utah. Brigham City's a fairsized town not far below the line, and there's a railhead there. What's more important, there are Mormons. Do you know about the Mormons?"

"I know that they are not like other white men," Yellow Wolf said, his eyes lighting with comprehension. "They do not use whiskey or tobacco or coffee, and they have as many wives as they want, which is sensible, and — "

"And they don't hate Indians and have never made war against 'em," Sundance said. "They think their mission is to convert them to their religion, not to kill them. But — " he grinned " — they do despise the American Army and the other Americans they call Gentiles. There are only two Army posts in Utah, and they're there not to protect the Mormons from Indians, but to watch the Mormons and protect the Gentiles from them."

He lit a cigarette with an ember from the fire. "Anyhow, the Mormons like money and they're honest. If we can

151

get the horses across the Utah line, I'll go down to Brigham City and hire Mormons to help us take them to the railroad and get them loaded. Then you and your braves can swing back through the mountains to Canada."

"But won't the Army try to stop me from shipping the horses when we come out in the open?" Doris asked.

"You'll have a bill of sale by then. As a British subject, they won't dare bother you or your property."

"And what about Drury?"

Sundance let smoke drift through his nostrils. "If Drury shows up," he said quietly, "I'll tend to him." He stood up. "There it is, Yellow Wolf. Help me get the horses out of Yellowstone Park and to the Utah boundary. Once there, if we can get the Mormons on our side, we won't need you any longer. They control the state, and once we're in Utah, we're safe. We can hire Mormons to go with the horses all the way east, for the matter, and see them on the ship, and if they undertake to do it, they'll do it."

"You make it sound so easy," Doris said wryly.

"It's not easy. Utah's our sanctuary, but before we get there, we've got maybe five hundred miles of the roughest country in the world to travel and the whole U.S. Army to dodge. Or, if it comes to that, fight."

Sitting Bull, who had been silent for a long time, said, "I think I can help, perhaps."

"How?"

The Sioux grinned. "Our young men are getting restless. A few sharp raids across the border on both sides of the Black Hills should draw a lot of soldiers off."

"Won't it make trouble for you with the Queen?"

"Who knows where they come from?"

When Sundance had translated this, Doris looked uneasy. "Jim, no. I won't have innocent people killed just to help me get those horses."

Sundance told this to Sitting Bull.

153

Bull nodded gravely. "Say this to her, Sundance. That it is not for the horses; my people would raid anyhow, it is only a matter of timing. And . . . innocent? When they have stolen a whole land from us and chased us from our homes to a strange country, killed our buffalo, imprisoned our warriors, killed our own women and children with their soldiers . . . how can it be that they are innocent?"

When he had said this, Doris did not answer; there was no answer possible. Yellow Wolf went to the teepee door.

"Sundance, when will you leave?"

"As soon as possible."

"By tomorrow just after sunrise," Yellow Wolf said, "I will have myself and fourteen other warriors, horses, guns, ammunition, and all necessary. Then we can ride." He turned, went out, and his voice, firm but still tinged with sadness, seemed to linger in the room for a moment after he had gone.

Sitting Bull also arose. "You and your woman have traveled far and you are tired. A lodge has been made ready for you and there is more food cooked. You are the guests of the Sioux. What we have is yours. Come." And he led the way and Sundance and Doris Bucknell followed.

# 6

IT was good, he thought, to be riding as an Indian again with such a party, the cool air from the mountains blowing sweet and fresh into his face, the laughter, joking, and constant watchfulness of the Nez Perce around him, his shield on his arm, his bow ready for action across his saddle, arrows clicking softly in the quiver on his shoulder with every movement of the big spotted stallion.

Except for the blue eyes, there was nothing left in his appearance of the white man. He had rubbed blacking in his hair until it was as dark as any Indian's; he wore a blanket coat with a hood; there were feathers in his hair and paint on his face. Beside him, also on a strong Appaloosa, Doris Bucknell was disguised as a warrior, too, her hair also blackened, a blanket around her

156

shoulders and over her head and face, her legs encased in buckskin leggings and moccasins, her cheeks, sunbronzed to a tan nearly as dark as an Indian, smeared with paint like his own. She carried no bow or shield, but there was a pistol on a belt around her waist, and she had fired a few practice rounds with it and Sundance saw that indeed she knew how to use it.

The disguises were necessary; the Northwest Mounted Police were like ghosts, materializing when least expected without warning. They would not question too much what seemed a hunting party of Nez Perce, but the presence of a white woman with such a band would have to be explained, and, besides, the reputation of Jim Sundance, the blond and blue-eyed Indian had spread this far north, and he would have also have to account for his presence in Canada.

And there was no arguing with the Mounties. Every Indian knew that. To defy or disobey one, much less to hurt or kill one, would bring prompt vengeance against the Sioux and cost them their sanctuary here. They had to be avoided, and when they could not be avoided, tricked.

They met, on their way south, one constable. In red coat and red pillbox hat, he traveled alone except for a packhorse on a long patrol. Fortunately, he was bound in the opposite direction; Sundance and Doris hung back with blankets muffling their faces, hiding their blue eyes, while Yellow Wolf respectfully explained that they were going to the mountains to hunt. Satisfied, the Mounted Policeman went on his way. Turning in his Indian saddle, Sundance watched the lonely scarlet dot vanish into the immensity of the country, and he felt a thrust of admiration. Yonder went a man.

They followed the Milk up to its headwaters, then swung south, and they were across the boundary line. Ahead, the Shining Mountains, the Rockies, divided into a dozen different smaller ranges, bulked against the sky, snow gleaming on the flanks of peaks. And now the ordeal really began.

Sundance led the way, for, better than any of them he knew this country, which had not been Nez Perce hunting grounds. And this was where the Appaloosas proved their worth.

They had to avoid the passes and the river valleys. To escape detection, it was necessary to keep to the flanks of the mountains, in thick timber, choose the roughest going, the places where no white men and probably no wandering Indians either would be. Where they traveled, nothing lived but mountain goats and sheep and eagles. And though this was summer, at night the cold was bitter.

Only the Appaloosas could have done it. Their legs were strengthened and their hoofs as hard as flint from a lifetime in the mountains, their big lungs especially adapted by years of selective breeding to extract the necessary oxygen from the thin, clear air. Their summer pelts were thicker than a lowland horse's, and proof against the cold. They knew how to live off the scant forage of the rocky slopes and deep woods, and most important of all, they had a mountain goat's sense of balance. More than once they traveled paths that made even Sundance's stomach knot and Doris, expert horsewoman that she was, cling tightly to her mount's mane and avert her eyes, but they rarely stumbled, if they did, recovered quickly, and never refused the challenge of a narrow ledge or dizzying jump.

And that, Sundance thought, was why the Nez Perce had stayed ahead of the Army for nearly two thousand miles. In fact, the soldiers would never have caught them in the Bear Paws if they had not thought they were already in safety across the Canadian border . . . No Army could catch the Appaloosas in their own country with Nez Perce in their saddles.

They sheltered under overhangs of

rock or in deep timber and were careful with their fires; they hunted with their bows for the sake of silence, but game was scarce at this altitude, and more than once they went hungry because there was no time for a long hunt, or because a rifle shot was too risky. It was a gruelling journey, rough on the men, and brutal for a woman. Yet, lying in Sundance's arms with their robes pulled over them at night, Doris Bucknell seemed strangely happy. "Jim," she whispered once, "what a magnificent adventure this is. What marvelous horses and horsemen. And what country! After this, England will seem so small and dull . . . I wish — " She broke off.

"What do you wish?"

"Never mind what I wish. It's impossible. Oh, I was going to say I wish I could stay here and not go home at all. But, of course, I must. I must see John's relatives, and there is his estate, his affairs, to be settled, so much to do, and I must be on hand to do it. And yet . . . Jim."

"Uhmhum?"

"Why don't you come with me? To England. After all, it was your father's home . . . "

"No," Sundance said. "This was his home. As soon as he saw this country, he knew this was what he had been looking for all his life. He gave up his family name, started absolutely fresh. He was the first white man ever allowed to join the sacred Sun Dance, and he took that for his name. No, this was his home, not England."

"England could be yours, though." She paused. "Jim, do you have any idea how enormously rich my husband was? And he had no brothers; most of it will come to me. You can't conceive of . . . well, it's many millions of your American dollars."

"I guessed it would be, since he could spend forty thousand on a whim. But what's that to do with me?"

"You . . . we . . . could live very well there, Jim. Anything you wanted, it could be yours. There would be no more fighting, no more danger, no more killing . . . a manor in the country in the summer, London in the season . . . and horses. The Appaloosas, and not only those, but all the others, you should see our stables, Jim. Our racers and hunters and hackneys and polo ponies; the Spanish barbs and the big Walers . . . " Her body pressed itself against his. "If you came home with me . . . "

Sundance was silent for a moment. "Doris, I'm sorry," he said at last.

She sighed. "I didn't really expect you to, but I had to try. You'd be a caged animal there, wouldn't you? You'd have to be a house cat when you've been a mountain panther all your life . . . "

"That's the size of it," Sundance said gently. "And I've got work to do here. It's more important to me than anything."

"Yes, I know that, I understand . . . " She laughed softly, with a touch of bitterness. "I guess I understand. And so I shall be happy with what I have now and make every moment count." Her hand moved across his body. "Every moment . . ."

They swung west and south of the Flathead Indian Reserve and after that the going was trickier and more risky. There was gold in this country, too much gold, and it had brought in white men, even to the most remote parts. Little towns that had not been there a year before studded the river valleys and the canyons: Yreka, McClellan's Gulch, Beartown and New Chicago. Each had to be scouted, bypassed, and the going was slow.

And then the Bannacks hit them.

There was no warning. Deep in the mountains, moving through a cold mist of twilight, they crossed a divide between two nameless creeks, came down a canyon where the sound of rushing water made a cold, constant thunder. On either side, sheer cliffs or

164

steep, rockstrewn slopes loomed above them. Yellow Wolf and a warrior named Bull Falling had scouted on ahead, found nothing, nor had Sundance expected them to. The place was so remote and barren, the going so rough and brutal, that no one not fugitives like themselves would be here. For once, knowing that soon they would camp, Sundance almost relaxed. He was content with their progress so far; with luck, another week would see them in the Park and in possession of the Nez Perce horses.

They went in single file along a narrow, uncertain trail beside the stream. Yellow Wolf rode in the lead, Bull Falling just behind, then Sundance and Doris Bucknell, and the others strung out behind.

Then Bull Falling, just in front of Sundance sighed strangely, twisted, pitched from his saddle. He had almost hit the ground before Sundance heard the thunder of the gun. For only one half second, he hesitated; then, as the canyon roared and boomed with the sound of many rifles, he wheeled Eagle, unslinging the Winchester looped to his saddle. Lead ricocheted, whining and zinging off of stone. "Take cover!" Sundance howled, and he left Eagle's saddle in a long jump, seizing Doris and dragging her along. She screamed as, savagely, he pulled her off the horse, threw her behind a rock, dived in on top of her, shielding her with his body. All around him bullets slapped and rang, and now he saw the powersmoke on the slope across the stream and on the rim almost above his head. They were trapped, whipsawed between two fires in the canyon.

Horses reared and plunged as their riders left their saddles, pulling them around to use as shields. Yet, which was surprising, none of the mounts went down. Sundance had no time to wonder at that as the Nez Perce took shelter wherever they could find it. It was up to him to cover them, and he edged around, got to his knees, sheltered by the rock, and opened fire on the marksmen across the way, firing at the plumes of smoke that betrayed their positions.

Then, from across the canyon, on the slope, there was a scream of agony, rising even above the answering thunder of Nez Perce guns. A figure lurched from a cleft in solid rock, turned, stumbled, then fell forward, rolled down the slope. Sundance stared unbelievingly. He had expected cavalry or maybe even Luke Drury and his men, but the dead man up there was an Indian.

There was no time to ponder that, they had to break this ambush. He tried to tally the number of guns against them: maybe five across the stream, maybe an equal number on the rim above.

"Stay down," he rasped at Doris. Shoving her to emphasize the order, he slipped his rifle into his arm's crook and crawled on his belly toward Yellow Wolf, forted up behind another pile of rocks, his rifle firing steadily. Despite all the lead thrown by the attackers, so far, save for Bear Falling, there had been no casualties that Sundance could see. Like many Indian, those up there were rotten riflemen. Crows, maybe, but this was not Crow range; the Blackfeet were better shots. Flatheads? They had no reason to fire on the Nez Perce. But, of course, there were the Bannacks —

Suddenly he knew. Bannacks hated Nez Perce and they were the worst shots he had ever seen. But what were they doing so far east? Their reservation was in Idaho, around Fort Hall, and they stuck close to it . . . Lead pranged around him, missing by a wide margin. Then he rolled behind Yellow Wolf's rock.

"Listen!" Sundance yelled above the gunfire. "They can't hit what they shoot at!"

"I know!" Yellow Wolf spat contemptuously. The Nez Perce were noted as the best marksmen in the West. Nor did they waste ammunition the way the attackers were doing. "I think they're Bannacks."

"So do I! Anyhow, give me three men and I'll clear that rim! Who're your best shots?"

"Tall Elk, Drum, Far Looker!" Yellow Wolf shouted the names. His voice, like a trumpet, rose above the sound of battle, and the three men ranged along the stream, snugged down in the rocks like so many lizards, looked toward him and caught Sundance's signal. They nodded as he pointed at the cliff above them.

It reared almost straight up, its wall sheer; indeed, there was a slight overhang which made it hard for the ambushers up there to fire straight down on the Nez Perce below. Whoever had chosen this spot for an ambush had either been a little stupid, hasty, or desperate. Anyhow, those men up there had to lean over the rim to get a clear shot.

Sundance moved out. Leaping from

behind the rock, he ran along the face of the cliff, dodging like a frightened panther, bent almost double. The other three came behind him, and the swirling twilight mist along the stream made them even harder targets. Then they had found new positions, and now they could fire up at the men on the rim as those leaned out to shoot. It was just a matter of being quick enough, accurate enough. Sundance, behind a massive boulder, raised his rifle, waited. The others spread out in cover behind him, followed suit. The canyon's rim was a jagged black line against the sky from this angle, and —

Sundance saw movement. He could shoot a grouse on the wing with a rifle, and the target he had now was not much bigger and just as quick. It was a gun-barrel with a man's head above it, silhouetted for the instant it took to fire.

The other three had seen it, too; four guns roared at once. That round silhouette literally exploded and a rifle dropped through space to smash on the rocks below. Sundance worked the lever of his Winchester, but the man called Drum saw the next target first. A single round, a scream, a man lurched to his feet, then spun down with flailing arms and legs.

Maybe three more, Sundance thought grimly. And they would be turning fire on this position. Meanwhile, the attackers on the far bank and Yellow Wolf traded constant fire, and Sundance heard a cry of pain from across the stream.

Then he saw it, a flicker of movement, come and gone in the uncertain light too swiftly for a shot. He fastened his eyes on the notch on the rim where it had been; again it came and went and still no target. Sundance grinned coldly. But the side of that notch was made of rock. That was bad luck for the man hiding in it. He loosed a stream of four quick rounds, heard them scream off stone. Then a hand fell from the notch, dangling motionless, with blood dripping from the fingers, and suddenly there was no more shooting from the rim at all. If there were two more men up there, they had decided to lie low.

"Watch the rim!" Sundance yelled at Drum, Tall Elk and Far Looker. Then, deliberately, he got to his feet. Lead from across the steam whined around him. He began to run, back towards Yellow Wolf. Up on the rim, somebody could not resist that target. His falling body nearly hit Sundance as it landed with a sickening crunch on the streamside rocks not ten feet away. Sundance flicked a glance a the corpse and knew he'd been right: a Bannack.

He made it back to Yellow Wolf. "The rim's clear!"

"Right! Cover me! I'm going across the creek!" Yellow Wolf leaped to his feet, gave a signal. Half a dozen Nez Perce rose and followed. Sundance and the rest poured fire into the rocks across the way, forcing the men there to keep to shelter as the Nez Perce plunged into the stream, rifles high.

It was a deadly business, crossing swift water over current-slickened rocks, but their moccasins found sure grips. They made it to the other bank, without casualties, spread out, running low through the mist. That mist shielded them until they were high on the slope above, and then it was brief and bloody, hand to hand. The five or so Bannacks there turned and tried to run. They never had a chance.

All at once, the canyon was strangely silent. No more gunfire echoed and re-echoed. If there were a Bannack left, he was on the rim, but more than likely he had fled.

Then a bloodcurdling sound rose from the slope over there. It was the war cry of Nez Perce counting coup on the bodies of the dead. Sundance peered through the mist. Now the Nez Perce were coming back down the slope. Then he let out a breath of satisfaction; they had taken a single prisoner. That was good. It was important to know why the Bannacks were here off their usual range and why they had attacked with such careless desperation.

Hands bound behind his back, knowing he was doomed, the Indian faced Sundance with stoic defiance. The Bannacks were a branch of Northern Paiute, and that was a language Sundance spoke. The man understood his questions all right, but he had made no answer since he had been brought back across the stream.

It was nearly dark, now; the horses had been gathered, the casualties counted. Bull Falling was dead; one Appaloosa had run away, but likely they would find it in the morning. Two other Nez Perce had taken minor wounds.

Sundance said, "I'll ask you one more time. Why were you here, why did you attack us? Where are your horses?"

Still silence. Yellow Wolf made a sound in his throat. "All right," he said hoarsely, "I'll take care of him. You remember, Sundance, at the battle of the Big Hole, how the Bannacks served as scouts against us. And afterwards, how they dug up the bodies of our women and children and what they did to them."

"I remember," Sundance said.

"Jim," Doris asked tensely, as Yellow Wolf drew a knife. "What — ?"

"Maybe you'd better not watch this."

"Torture?"

Sundance said, "Revenge."

"Even so, will he tell you what you need to know?"

"I doubt it. Likely he'll die without a word — when he does die."

"Then why don't you let him go?"

Sundance stared at her.

"Maybe he's not afraid of torture. But maybe he wants to live. Maybe he'd trade you the information for his life. This way, he has no hope of living no matter what."

Sundance drew in a long breath. "Do you know what, Doris? Sometimes I'm almost too much Indian for my own good." He turned to Yellow Wolf. "Wait."

The Nez Perce looked at him blankly. Sundance spoke rapidly in Paiute. Slowly the Bannack's face changed. But Yellow Wolf, who also understood the language, was enraged. Sundance had to talk swiftly, with all the authority at his command. Presently, Yellow Wolf spat, turned away, and sheathed the knife. Then a cascade of words sluiced from the Bannack.

Sundance listened closely, and as he did, his heart sank. When the man was through, he drew his own Bowie with a swift motion. The Bannack's eyes widened, but Sundance only spun him around, slashed his ropes. For one astounded second the Bannack stood there. Then he began to run. Yellow Wolf whirled, raising his rifle. Sundance knocked it up. "I gave a promise to him!" he roared. "Let him go! He doesn't count, now! Maybe nothing counts, now!"

As the Bannack vanished into the mist, Yellow Wolf sucked in a long breath. "I did not want to hear his filthy voice. What did he say?" His tone was saner.

All the Nez Perce were listening intently now.

"He said," Sundance answered, "that there's no way we can get to the Nez Perce horses. In fact, unless the Army's blind, it's likely found them by now."

For a moment, there was nothing but the sound of rushing water in the canyon. Then, after he had wearily translated this for Doris, she said, unbelievingly, "Found them?"

Sundance was suddenly very tired and he sat down on a rock. "The one thing I wasn't counting on was another Indian war in the same territory. But it's happened. While we were bound for Canada, the Bannacks went off their reservation in Idaho, killed some whites, and — It's almost the Nez Perce thing all over, except that the Bannacks aren't the soldiers the Nez Perce are.

They've already been whipped a couple of times, and they're scattered and spread out from here to Idaho. The whole American Army's out against them, moving into these mountains from every side. The Bannacks that we just fought — they tried to use our old trail through Yellowstone Park. There were soldiers everywhere. They had to turn around and run again, and they wore out their horses. That's why they tried to take us, to get fresh mounts. But . . . if what he says is true, and it sounded true, the soldiers are patrolling the whole trail across the Absarokas. They're checking every side canyon and cut off and there's no hiding place to hide, he said, and that means, by now — " He broke off. "I was a fool," he said dully. "I was a fool to hide them there. I should have taken them up to Canada."

Yellow Wolf looked down at his moccasins. "You could not know. If you had taken them to Canada, the Army would have asked the Queen

178

to give them back, and maybe she would have. They would have been safe in the Absarokas if only — Last year, the Bannacks helped the soldiers against our people. Who would think that this year they would turn and fight them? It is not your fault. It is *Wyakin*, the great power, Fate. But . . . What should we do now?" He was shivering with cold from his wet clothes.

Sundance looked down the mountain stream, mind working swiftly, checking the alternatives. At last he said, "You and your people and the woman hide. We'll pick a safe place tomorrow, and if you have to leave there while I'm gone, leave me a sign to say where; I'll find it."

"While you're gone? Gone where?"

Sundance rubbed his hand through his hair, looked at the blacking on his palm. "I've got to travel as a white man again for a while. I'm going into town, I think Virginia City at Alder Gulch. I'll hear the news there and find out what has happened and where the

179

soldiers are. If the horses have already been found, they will know that too."

"And if they have?"

"Sooner or later," Sundance said, "the Army will turn them over to Drury. Once they have them actually in their hands, they will pay no money to Joseph for them, either. Drury will take them to his stud farm in Oregon and — "

Yellow Wolf raised his head, and his eyes lit again. "And it's a long trip from here to Oregon," he said. "If we can strike their trail . . . " He sucked in his breath. "It is a long time since I have been on a raid to steal some horses. That will be much pleasure. Especially since the horses are our own."

"That's the idea," Sundance said. "Now, we need a better place to camp. Let's ride."

## 7

IT sprawled across one of the richest gulches in the world, but now it was beginning to run down as most mining towns did when the easy-to-mine placer gold was exhausted. They had been digging gold out of Alder Gulch since the early 1860's, and until last year Virginia City had been the capital of Montana Territory. That had been moved to Helena, now, but there was still life left in the rip-roaring collection of log huts and frame houses and every other building was still a saloon that ran around the clock. Sundance rode in at midday, his hair yellow again, his dress as it had been when he had left Deadwood, the Colt lowslung around his waist, his Winchester across the bow of a stock saddle borrowed from one of the Indians who had taken it as loot during the long retreat. As always, people watched him with curiosity, for he stood out even in the motley crowd of this mining camp, and he watched them with equal alertness and curiosity. He was not surprised to see a lot of blue uniforms vivid among the flannel shirts of the miners. The Bannack had been right in that respect; the mountains were alive with soldiers; he had dodged two patrols coming in.

He knew the town, of course, and his first destination was the office of the Montana *Democrat*, its newspaper. The woman behind the counter in the unimposing office was startled at the sight of the blond, blue-eyed halfbreed, and even more startled when he bought a newspaper and quickly read it. Having digested what it contained, Sundance threw it back on the counter and left.

The news, of course, was several days old, but it verified everything told him by the Bannack. The Bannacks had signed a treaty with the Government which gave them the stretch of land

182

called Camas Prairie. The camas root, growing there in abundance, was a staple of the diet of the Northwestern Indians, and once the Nez Perce had claimed it as their own. Anyhow, a clerical error in the treaty document listed the land as "Kansas Prairie," and, taking advantage of that, white settlers had moved in.

The same old story, Sundance thought bitterly. The Bannacks had scouted for the Army against the Sioux and Nez Perce, but the whites had no qualms about betraying even their closest Indian allies. Enraged, Buffalo Horn, the Bannack chief, had killed some settlers and jumped the reservation. Most of the fighting had taken place in Oregon and Idaho, but some of the badly beaten Indians had tried to retreat across the mountains to Montana. The Department of the Platte had moved out troops to block the passes, especially the trails the Nez Perce had used the year before. The question was, had they found the horses and if so, where had they taken them?

As in any other Western town, the real source of up to date news was the saloons. The next move was to make the rounds, keep his ears open.

There was plenty to hear, but most of it was rumor or downright hysteria, the kind always generated among the whites by any Indian outbreak. There were the usual bored drunks wanting to form a militia and go out and kill some redskins — any redskins, soldiers, plenty of them, boasting about exploits that had never happened, and yet, amidst it all, there was also a definite undercurrent of sympathy for the Bannacks. They had not earned it; it had been earned for them by the Nez Perce a year ago. On their long retreat Joseph had, by and large, held his column to the rules of civilized warfare and he had tried hard to negotiate a peaceful journey through Montana. The skill with which he and his war chiefs, Jim Sundance among them, had outwitted the Army time after time, or wiped its nose in battle, had earned admiration even from the whites; so had his nobility in defeat. Now that the Indians were no longer strong enough even to present a real threat of reclaiming their stolen land, the whites could allow themselves an understanding of their feelings and their motives.

Most of all, though, Sundance watched the soldiers. If the horses had not been found, the word would still have been out: get Jim Sundance, the halfbreed with the yellow hair. But if the Army had them, then all interest in him would probably have been lost. The soldiers in the bars paid him little or no attention, and a certainty began to build in him . . .

His technique was to buy a beer, sit a long time over it, listening, leave most of it behind. He was still clearheaded and cold sober when, in the fifth saloon, a big man in a leather jacket and buckskin pants and high jack boots

185

detached himself from the bar and came toward him as he entered. With long brown hair and keen brown eyes and a heavy mustache, the man was white, though his skin was sunbronzed. His voice was soft and almost cultured. "Hello, Jim," he said. "I thought you'd show up where the action was." He put out his hand.

"Luther," Sundance said.

"Let's have a beer. Been wanting to talk to you since the Nez Perce trouble last year. I'm glad you got clear before the surrender." Luther Kelly, usually called Yellowstone Kelly, gestured to a table.

Sundance nodded and they took chairs and Kelly signaled for two beers. Yellowstone Kelly was, with Hickok dead and Cody in the east, perhaps the best white scout in the West now. Unlike most frontiers-men, he rarely drank, had little taste for carousing; he was thoughtful and a great reader. He was also, as Sundance well knew, hell in a fight. He had been Chief of

Scouts for Miles throughout the Nez Perce war. He and Sundance had been on opposite sides then, but they had worked together in the past, and they liked and trusted each other.

"If you're aiming to join the Bannacks," Kelly said, "they're pretty well whipped. You're too late, Jim."

Sundance only shrugged. Let Kelly think that was what drew him to this region. The beer came and both men toyed with it. Then Kelly said, almost casually, "And that might not be the only thing you're too late for."

Sundance sat up straight. "Meaning?"

Kelly looked thoughtfully at his beer. "You know, I've gone out against a lot of Indians in my time. But I never really hated to win a battle against 'em until last year in the Bear Paws when Joseph came in. That speech he made . . . " He leaned back, quoting. "'I am tired of fighting . . . Our chiefs are killed . . . He who led the young men is dead . . . It is cold and we have no blankets. The little children are freezing to death. My people . . . have run away to the hills . . . no one knows where . . . perhaps freezing to death. I want time to look for my children and see how many of them I can find. Perhaps I will find them among the dead. Hear me, my chiefs. I am tired; my heart is sick and sad. From where the sun now stands, I will fight no more forever.'"

After that he was silent for a moment, as Sundance looked at him. Kelly smiled then, a little shyly. "I memorized it." Then he was serious. "Jim, that was a war that should never have been fought. Of all the Indians out here, the Nez Perce, to me, have always seemed the greatest. And then, when they were double-crossed, when, instead of sending 'em back to Lapwai, Miles loaded them on the flat-boats . . . " He drew in a long breath. "Damn," he said. "I felt dirty."

Sundance only spread his hands.

"It can't be undone, of course," Kelly said, "and it's made me a big man in these parts, a kind of hero. But I never have taken much to the hero role. Ever since that surrender, I've wished that there was something I could do to . . . well, make up for what happened." Then he took a swallow of beer. "By the way, did you know that the Army found a herd of Nez Perce horses hidden in the Absarokas two weeks ago?"

Sundance looked at Kelly without a flicker of expression. "Did they, now."

"Yep." Kelly drank again. "Six of the most magnificent stallions you ever saw and a bunch of mares and foals. Hidden in the damnest valley you ever saw. Two Nez Perce guarding them, but the Army rubbed them out."

Sundance's hands clamped hard around the beer glass.

Kelly went on, still carefully casual. "In fact, the trail in and out was so bad that they had to call in a civilian to get those horses out. Maybe you've heard of a man named Luke Drury. I'll say this for him, he's a master horseman. Me, I'd have sworn they needed wings to get out of there, but he managed it somehow. Lost one foal, that's all."

"So," Sundance said. "Then what became of them?"

"They played the old Army game," Kelly said. "The Army took title to them as spoils of war. Then, I understand, they sold them to Drury for some ridiculous price. He's a remount contractor, you know. I understand he's taking 'em back to Oregon." His eyes narrowed. "Me, I'd have said they belonged to Chief Joseph. That the Army should have dickered with him and paid him a fair price. But, of course, you know how it works."

"I know how it works," Sundance said. "Drury passes money under the table, buys 'em for a song, some officer makes a big deposit. Then he breeds Appaloosas for remounts and the Army buys 'em from him and he gets rich. So do the purchasing officers. Yeah, I know exactly how it works." He looked down at his beer. "To Oregon, eh? I wonder what trail he aims to follow."

"Why, the easiest one, I'm sure," Kelly said firmly.

Sundance considered. "That would be up through Bozeman to Helena, and then by Hellgate Pass over to Missoula."

Kelly nodded. "Follow the wagon road to Walla-Walla, cut off to Pierce City across the Bitterroots in Idaho, then to Lapwai and on down the Wallowa Valley, Joseph's old home, into Oregon. He'll make good time, too." Kelly's eyes flicked to Sundance's face then away. "He left Bozeman three days ago. Four more and he'll be deep in the Bitterroots."

Sundance began to roll a cigarette. "With a big cavalry escort, I reckon."

"No," Kelly said. "They didn't go that far. But he don't need one. He's got about twenty of the toughest gunslingers I've ever laid eyes on. He must have combed every hellcamp in the Northwest for 'em. Said he wasn't takin' any chances of losin' those spotted stallions. I don't reckon he will. It would take a lot of fightin' men to pry 'em loose from him."

Sundance did not answer. "Me," Kelly went on, "I've never taken much of a shine to Drury. I took even less of one when I saw what he did to one of those Nez Perce guardin' the herd."

"Which was?"

"Well, the Army killed one outright. Another one, named Dead Man Walking, took a bad wound. He was still alive when Drury reached the valley. And Drury had a notion that this Nez Perce had some information he wanted — about a man named Jim Sundance." Kelly paused. "He wanted Dead Man Walking to admit that Jim Sundance had fought with the Nez Perce and that it was Sundance who'd brought the horses there. Seems like Drury had a big mad-on against you, Jim. Wanted some kind of leverage to get you slung in prison."

"Go on," Sundance said harshly. "About Dead Man Walking."

"Well, he died," Kelly answered. "The soldiers turned their heads and left him with Drury and he died hard. But he never talked. I wasn't there when it happened, but I saw the body. What was left of it, I mean. He used fire. A lot of fire. It went all over me, and I started to look him up myself, but he was gone."

"I see." Sundance felt no grief, only white hot rage.

"But, like I said, it'll take a lot of fightin' men ever to git those horses away from Drury. If anybody does, me, I hope it's somebody that can use 'em for Chief Joseph some way." He drained his glass. "Anyhow, that's the news, Jim."

"Why, I appreciate you bringing' me up to date, Luther. Let me buy you a drink."

"One beer's my limit. Anyhow, I got to ride south tomorrow. Just happenstance I took a break to come to Virginia City. Never expected to see you here, but I'm glad I did." He shoved back his chair. "Real glad."

Sundance arose and they shook hands. "One more thing, Luther. Am I wanted?"

"You were, before, for questioning. Now . . . not officially. Still, I don't know of anybody that more people would rather have his scalp than you. So watch yourself, Jim."

"I aim to," Sundance said. "See you, Luther. And thanks again." He turned, strode from the saloon. There was no need to stay longer here. Mounting Eagle, he headed out of town. As soon as he was clear of Virginia City, he turned northwest, riding hard.

# 8

EIGHTEEN hours later, Sundance found the Nez Perce where he had left them, in a lost canyon heavily wooded, jagged with rock outcroppings, threaded with streams, and with just enough grass to restore the strength of the spotted horses. Eagle stumbled as he went down the treacherous canyon floor; Sundance had asked the very maximum of the big horse, and the stallion had given it. But now his head hung low with weariness, his great flanks heaved, and he trembled with the chill of the thick lather drying on him. Sundance himself swayed in the saddle with weariness, and he had rubbed tobacco into his eyes to keep them open. But he had made it. Now, perhaps, there might just be barely time.

He was challenged at the canyon

mouth by Drum and Far Looker. They steadied him with a hand on each arm and led him into an offshoot of the canyon, where the Nez Perce had their camp.

"Jim!" Doris' voice rang out, and she jumped up from beside the fire and ran toward him.

"Somebody take care of Eagle," Sundance said. "I'll be all right." He almost fell off the horse, and he swayed as Doris embraced him, then led him to the fire. Yellow Wolf and the others crowded up, as Sundance dropped on to spread robes and Doris handed him a chunk of roasted venison.

The Nez Perce were tense, but with instinctive courtesy asked no questions until he had eaten, the meat sending new strength through him. "What have you learned?" blurted Yellow Wolf at last.

Sundance told him, about the horses and about what Drury had done to Dead Man Walking. Yellow Wolf's face seemed to turn to metal; it was like something moulded out of hardened copper, but he did not speak. "And there it is," Sundance said. "Drury's taking the horses west and south down through Idaho to Oregon. He's got the advantage; he can travel good roads and make good time. And there are twenty gunmen with him. Somehow, we have to stop him before he gets so far in Idaho that he's under Army protection. The best time to hit him would be when he crosses the Bitterroots. He'll be alone up on the Divide, then."

Yellow Wolf closed his eyes, and Sundance knew that, behind them, he was seeing a map of the country. For a moment, an unmasked flicker of despair crossed the Nez Perce's face. "Can we do it? If we were eagles, it would be an easy trip. But we are not eagles, and must stay off the main trails and climb many mountains."

"We've got to do it," Sundance said. "Somehow."

"Jim." Doris took his hand. "Jim, maybe the horses aren't worth it. He has so many gunmen, you said. Are they worth these men dying to get them back? They've cost so much already — John and . . . "

"They're worth it," Sundance said. "Without that second twenty thousand, a lot more Nez Perce will die in Kansas this winter than we'll lose here. But that aside, it's something else. Those aren't Drury's horses, they aren't the Army's horses, they're the Nez Perce horses, and, by God, they're entitled to have them back to dispose of as they see fit. Besides, you heard what he did to Dead Man Walking . . . "

"Yes," she said.

"So it can't be stopped. It's a blood debt, one Drury has to pay. But you . . . I can leave you in Virginia City or some such town now, and you'll be safe. You can meet us in Utah at Brigham City and — "

"No!" she snapped. "I'm not leaving you!"

"Doris, you don't know what kind of ride it's gonna be — We've got to go full speed across country just as rough as what we've come through, dodge the soldiers, maybe fight 'em, get through somehow before he gets too deep in Idaho, and it's gonna take everything every horse and man has got."

"All the same, I'm going," she said. She stood up. "I'm a good enough horsewoman to make it, you've seen that. And . . . All right. If it comes down to blood debts, I've got one to collect from Drury myself. More than one . . . " And he knew she was thinking of what Drury must have done to her that night in the Deadwood cabin.

"All right," Sundance said. "You're sure entitled to it. And you say you can use a gun. We'll need every gun we've got, even yours." Then he broke off, for Yellow Wolf was speaking.

"There is a chance," Yellow Wolf said. "It's a long one, but — " He began to rattle off a route. Sundance listened closely; he knew this country, but not like Yellow Wolf. To the Nez

Perce, every fold and wrinkle, peak and valley, lake and river, was as familiar as his own mother's face. "It will push the horses to the very limit," Yellow Wolf said. "Us, too. But maybe . . . just maybe we can make the pass where the road crosses the Bitterroots Divide in time to catch him there. If we could, then it would be easy to fade into the mountains with the horses . . . We'll try it; we'll leave at first light tomorrow, and anyone who can't keep up must stay behind." He looked at the girl.

"She'll keep up," said Sundance. "I'll see to that. I'll give her Eagle."

The sun was still behind the mountains, mist hanging low in the canyon when they struck out the next morning, with Yellow Wolf in the lead. Their route would take them through such wild and rugged country that there was little fear of soldiers except in one or two crucial spots. A night's rest had restored Eagle; he was fresh and strong under Doris and Sundance knew he could get the most out of her previous mount, a smaller horse.

It was a wilderness, a jumbled, magnificent one. Ahead loomed the Continental Divide, which they had already crossed one time, slowly, a barrier running almost east-west here. They could not afford the time to go back the way they had come; this time they would take Lost Trail Pass and hope it was not blocked by soldiers. That would bring them out in the Bitterroots, with a good seventy miles of rugged mountains still to traverse.

The great spotted stallions were in their element, and they had to be, for they were pushed mercilessly, granted only enough rest to keep them going. Sundance had been on many a forced march with Indians and cavalry both, but never like this. Without the Appaloosas, there would have been no chance at all.

The first day, they rode for twenty hours. Even after the sun went down, they kept on, for the Nez Perce and their horses could see in the dark almost like cats. By then, Doris was exhausted; sometimes Sundance steadied her in the saddle. Yet, she hung on, grimly, and he was full of admiration for her when, finally, Yellow Wolf called a halt. His judgement of her had been correct; she was a thoroughbred.

Four hours sleep, that much rest and graze for the spotted horses, and then they were on their way again, toiling up the Continental Divide, the Shining Mountains magnificent against the sky on their left flank, and ahead. Those mountains were both friend and enemy, shielding them from discovery by the Army, but every foot of steepness costing precious time and strength. Again the horses achieved the impossible, toward evening they broke out at Lost Trail Pass, carefully scouted in advance and found to be clear of soldiers. Despite her weariness, Doris made a sound of awe and delight at the spectacle spread out below them, a huge wilderness, shagged with timber, jeweled with green valleys, threaded with silver streams, all struck by the rays of the sinking sun.

But they wasted no time looking at the scenery. They went on, turning into the high country of the Bitterroots. Although it was only late summer, it was snowing when Yellow Wolf halted them again, long after dark. The Nez Perce made no comment, but Sundance sensed his apprehension. If this turned into one of the raw summer blizzards that sometimes came at this altitude . . . But maybe if it did, it would slow down Drury, too.

Drury. At the thought, Sundance's weariness vanished. He remembered that slugging boot toe in his ribs; he thought of Dead Man Walking, who had been his friend, and of Joseph waiting in Kansas for some word, wondering whether his people could survive the winter and buy their way home again in the spring. It was a while before, with Doris against him in the robes under the shelter of a cliff, he could get to sleep.

By dawn, the snow had stopped; not enough to slow their progress. The Nez Perce made their morning prayers of gratitude; Sundance joined them. Then they rode.

Now they traveled the very spine of the Bitterroots, following game trails through timber, dropping down when they could into easier valleys, crossing saddle and climbing peaks. The Appaloosas were not made of steel, and they showed the strain. Each man desperately needed a fresh mount, and, of, course, there was none; there was no alternative save to ride them to death if it came to that to catch Drury before he got out of the mountains. There would be not only the Appaloosa breeding band but the mounts of Drury's men to replace them. And yet, Sundance felt the agony of Eagle's exhaustion as keenly as his own. He and his big warhorse had been together for a long time; it was more than mount, it was friend, companion, and guardian, and he loved the big stallion. But he would sacrifice it, if there were no other way.

The men were equally worn out, all riding in a fog. Some fell asleep in their saddles. Sundance and Yellow Wolf stayed awake, always out on the point, and somehow Doris managed to keep up with them.

When the sun was halfway down the sky, they rested. Yellow Wolf looked at it, then at the wilderness ahead, and his face was grave. "Tomorrow," he said. "If your information was right, he could cross the pass tomorrow. And there's no way we can make it before tomorrow night."

Sundance said, "We can only do the best we can and hope. If he beats us to the pass, we'll have to catch up with him and fight him down below, Army or no Army. Let's ride on."

They did, but it was absolutely necessary to stop at sundown, or there would have been no horses to mount on the following day. There had been no time to hunt, and their food had run out. But in their weariness, they ignored the pangs of hunger and slept like logs. In the morning, Sundance awakened to see a black-tailed deer not a hundred yards away, in full view, on a mountainside, staring at them curiously. He sat up slowly, reaching for his bow beside his robes; Doris and the Nez Perce were still sound asleep.

The deer's ears flicked, it snorted. Sundance deftly strung the bow, found an arrow. The deer raised its head a little, tensed, as he pulled the feather to his cheek. Then it sprang high in the air, came down running. Sundance jumped up, ran after it, as it disappeared in heavy timber. Twenty yards farther on in the woods, he found it dead, the arrow almost buried behind its left foreleg. Fingers numb with cold, he dragged the carcass back to camp: the Nez Perce were already gobbling parts of it raw when he began to cook some for Doris and himself.

And they rode on; and the horses

were fresher now, and the men no longer dozed; they were wide awake and alert, nerved up. For this was the last day, the day of decision. Late evening, if they pushed the horses to the limit, should bring them to where the road from Missoula crossed the Bitterroots, to the place of reckoning with Luke Drury. If only he had not beat them to it, if only he were not already halfway down the range into the more thickly settled parts of Idaho . . .

By three o'clock, the horses were worn out again, but every minute counted now. Their riders forced them through a stand of timber so thick there was hardly room for them to pass, and their flanks and chests were raw and bleeding when they emerged, but they went on, their gallantry, like their iron strength, bred into them by generations of men like Yellow Wolf, knowledgeable and loving and prepared to take infinite pains to improve the herd.

"Jim," Doris gasped, swaying in the

207

saddle. "Jim, for heaven's sake, aren't we almost there?"

"Almost," Sundance said. "Maybe an hour more. Hang on."

"Don't worry. I'm hanging on."

Sundance put his mount into a trot, came up alongside Yellow Wolf. "If we're lucky, if they haven't crossed the pass, we'll wait and take them in the morning. They won't cross at night."

Yellow Wolf nodded.

"And remember," Sundance said. "Drury, the tall white man with two guns and the broken nose. He is mine." He paused. "I have told all of you. If at all possible, I want him alive."

Yellow Wolf smiled. "To deal with him like he dealt with Dead Man Walking? I have some ideas that you can use."

"Maybe that. But first I have to have a paper from him before I can ship the horses."

Yellow Wolf looked at him in surprise. "A paper?"

"Saying that he sells them to the

woman. That the Nez Perce horses belong to her. One that the white men will honor. Otherwise, the Mormons will not help us."

"That they belong to her. Yes, I see." Yellow Wolf's face shadowed. "I had forgotten. But this is true. After the fight, they will belong to her."

"And Joseph's people will stay alive."

Yellow Wolf nodded, but he rode on ahead in silence.

Sundance kept pace behind him, watching him with foreboding. And yet, he could not believe Yellow Wolf would break a promise to him . . .

Then the Nez Perce reined in. "There," he said. "Beyond that rise. The road runs there."

Ahead, the ground humped itself, thickly furred with lodgepole pines. Sundance nodded. "Tell the others to stay here; you and I will go down and scout."

They faded into the lodgepoles and Sundance and Yellow Wolf rode on. Just below the crest, Sundance pulled up. "I think we'd better go ahead on foot."

He slid off the Appaloosa, rifle in hand, bow and quiver over his shoulder. Yellow Wolf followed suit, and they ran silently through the timber, taking to cover. They edged over the rise, looked down the slope, and below they could see the road.

In the East, it would have been no road at all. It was merely a wide trail, showing the old ruts of occasional wagon passage, winding through a clearing in the timber where the mountains fell away to a gap. It appeared to be deserted, and then Sundance and Yellow Wolf looked at one another and went carefully down the hill in leaps and bounds, each covering the other. They reached the edge of the timber, and they halted there in the shelter of the trees.

There was no sound save the wind in the pines, and if there had been a herd of horses with twenty outriders on either side of the pass, Sundance and Yellow Wolf would have heard them. All the same, Sundance took no chances. "Cover me," he said.

Yellow Wolf nodded, gun up. Sundance eased down the gentle, wooded slope, took another good look, stepped out into the road. His heart hammered with suspense as he bent to examine the narrow track. Like a questioning hound, he ran, hunched over, a few yards in either direction. Then he let out a long breath and came back to where Yellow Wolf waited tensely, a question in his eyes.

"They haven't crossed yet," Sundance said.

"They had time to. Maybe your white friend lied."

"Kelly didn't lie, I'll swear to that. He made damned sure I knew exactly what route Drury would take. More likely Drury got hung up in some town along the way. But he'll be along, unless he's changed his plans without Kelly's knowledge. He's probably already camped farther down the pass, in better shelter."

"Maybe we should go after him and take him tonight. It would be easier in the dark."

Sundance shook his head. "Our horses aren't in shape, and neither are we, after that ride. Besides, some of 'em might get away in the dark. We don't want that." He gestured. "This is as good a place to set up our ambush as any. Plenty of cover on both sides of the road, and high ground. We'll post men on each side, right away and send outposts down the trail to warn us when he comes. We'll have no fire tonight, and we want to leave our horses further back and on the forward slope, so the herd Drury drives can't get wind and alert him. Doris can bring them up when the shooting starts in case we need 'em."

Yellow Wolf nodded, but, an experienced fighting man himself, withheld judgment until he had also looked over the ground once more. Then he said, "You're right. It shall be as you say."

The night before a battle was always the same, Sundance thought, whether the combatants were white or red. There was a grim tension, each man wondering inwardly whether he would be alive at sundown tomorrow and each dealing with his fear in his own way. White soldiers would have been writing home, but even if the Nez Perce had been able to write, they no longer had a home. Their families were scattered all across the West, those whose families had not been killed. Mothers, fathers, brothers, sisters — some lay in unmarked graves or were only gnawed bones in the wilderness. Others were in Canada or at Lapwai in Idaho, or in Kansas with Chief Joseph, or maybe wandering still somewhere else. So they dealt with their tensions in their own way. Some laughed, joked; others were moodily silent, and many, exhausted, slept.

For Sundance, however, there was no sleep for a long while. He and Yellow Wolf disposed the men on either side of the road with meticulous care and made sure each knew what he was to do. They sent scouts down the pass, eastward, to watch and give them warning.

"Jim," Doris said. "You need to rest."

"Later."

"Jim, what's wrong? You've come this far — "

Sundance hesitated, and then he voiced his fear. "This far. And suppose it's a wild goose chase? Suppose Kelly was wrong, or he did lie to me?"

"You said he wouldn't do that."

"I thought he wouldn't. But there have been so many betrayals . . . " Sundance sat down on the robes beside her, drawing a blanket around him against the night chill. "For the Nez Perce, it's been one big betrayal after another. And they haven't deserved any of them."

He paused. "I'm half Cheyenne, and I think the Cheyennes are the greatest people in the world. But if I weren't

Cheyenne, I would want to be Nez Perce. The high country they have always lived in is a kind of paradise. Plenty of game, plenty of food plants, the camas, the bitterroot, the cowish; they had no reason to make war or hate anybody until the white men came. In fact, they have always lived more like white men than most other Indians, and have always dealt with them on more equal terms, and have understood them better. They took to the missionaries when they came, and old Joseph, young Joseph's father, didn't split away until the first treaty they made was broken. Then he got disgusted, went back to the old religion, took his band to the Wallowa valley. All he wanted was to be left alone —— "

Sundance looked toward the bank of Appaloosas, which she must bring up when the shooting started, if it ever did. "They were breeding horses by the kind of methods you used in England when Lewis and Clark first came. And as soon as they could buy cattle from the emigrants, they started herds of their own. They made no war on whites, and they warred against the other tribes only to defend their land. If there ever was a tribe of Indians who could have lived in peace with the whites, it was the Nez Perce. But the white people wouldn't let them."

He paused. "Year before last, they found gold in the Wallowa valley, Joseph's country. White settlers came in. They laid on the political pressure. Then the Government told the Nez Perce the treaty had to be rewritten. They designated one of the Christian chiefs as spokesman for the whole tribe and pressured his signature on the paper. Then they told Joseph he had to give up his land and come in to Lapwai. He hated that, but finally he consented. He took his people back into the mountains to round up their horses and cattle for the move."

Sundance's voice was bitter. "The young men weren't happy. Two of them had lost relatives, shot down by white men as if they were deer or some other kind of game. A few of them went on a raid and killed the men who had shot their people. That tore it. Joseph knew there'd be trouble. He gathered his people and decided to go east and seek refuge with the Crows, who were also friends of the white men and old friends of the Nez Perce. The Army went out against them, and the Nez Perce outran the Army and outfought it. They traveled halfway across Montana, and mostly there was no trouble with the whites, they even traded with them. Some white men got killed, yes, the young men are always hard to hold. They sought help from the Flatheads, who were nearer, but the Flatheads, also old friends, betrayed them, wouldn't take them in. Neither would the Crows. So they decided to do what Sitting Bull had done and go to Canada. They thought they were across the line when Nelson Miles hit them with artillery. He blew the hell out of them, killed an awful lot because he wanted complete credit for the victory, wanted to make sure Joseph surrendered before General Howard could come up to take the surrender and the credit. Joseph surrendered because he thought they would be sent back to Lapwai to join the others. Instead of that, Sheridan wired Miles to send them to Kansas. Miles took their horses and loaded them on flatboats and sent 'em down the river. Believe it or not, in Bismarck, Dakota Territory, the whites gave a testimonial dinner for Joseph. They admired him that much. He had a lot of white people on his side, but that cut no ice with the Army. The whole Indian problem is in their hands now, and they've got their own rough way of handling it. So . . . " He spread his palms. "The Government betrayed Joseph. The Army betrayed him. The Flatheads and the Crows, whom he thought were his friends, betrayed him. Only Sitting Bull and the Sioux, who used to be the bitter enemy of the Nez Perce, took them in, gave them refuge. Now, they trust no one. Why should they? They're not savages, they're intelligent human beings, but even so — You can only ask a man to stand for so much."

He looked toward the road. "They're waiting for that now — their revenge for all they've endured. I've promised it to them. And I've promised them that they'll regain their horses. Only for a little while, yes; you'll take them to England. But at least they'll dispose of them themselves. But — "

He stood up.

"I've led them back and forth across the mountains. I've made them promises. And then . . . suppose Drury doesn't come? All that pent-up rage, that hatred . . . I'm not afraid for myself. But, you — If they don't have Drury to explode on, they'll turn against you and me. And . . . "

"And I wouldn't blame them," Doris said. She was silent for a moment. Then she said, "It was all a game with us, you see? Just another of John's hobbies. It would be so interesting to come to America, meet red Indians, buy their horses. We didn't know what was behind it, what the horses meant to these people. All we knew was that we were rich, and that we wanted something they had and we could afford to buy it . . . " She clasped her hands. "John was that way. He used money the way he used a sword when he was in the cavalry. But it was all a game to him, war, polo, the Nez Perce horses . . . Entertainment, amusement. He did not feel deeply about them."

Suddenly, she stood up. "Excuse me, Jim."

Sundance stared at her. "Where are you going?"

Yellow Wolf speaks a little English, doesn't he?"

"More than a little."

"And I speak a little Nez Perce. All right. I'll be back after a while. I want to see him. Don't try to follow me."

Sundance said, "Doris — "

But she had already swung up on Eagle, bareback, gathering his picket rope in her hand for a rein. She was a superb rider, and before Sundance could stop her, she had put the spotted stallion into a gallop. He watched her disappear into the woods, headed toward the ambush at the pass, where Yellow Wolf was, for the night, in command. Sundance stood there for a moment, and then, to relieve the tension, he took the marijuana from his parfleche and made a cigarette and smoked it.

He lay in the robes when she came back.

"Doris — "

"Don't ask me any questions, Jim." She climbed into the robes beside him. "Just, for now, make love to me."

Sundance rolled over. "Yes," he said.

# 9

THE sun was high, the sky clear, the mountains shining in its light. It was a fine day, a magnificent day, and at ten o'clock in the morning a scout came in with the news that Drury was on his way.

It was Drum, and his eyes were shining with excitement, as he found Sundance. "Our horses! You were right! They come! They are a half hour down the pass, all the stallions, all the mares, and the young foals! They come very slowly because of the foals."

"I should have thought of that." Now Sundance knew how they had gained the extra time. But a great knot within him seemed to unloose itself: he had been right, the gamble had paid off.

"There are twenty men, about, exactly as you said," Drum went on, lying beside Sundance in the pines. "They are fighters, too. Many guns, many, many guns. Six of them ride ahead to scout the pass and draw our fire if we are here."

"All right," Sundance said. "Go across the road and tell Yellow Wolf. And say I will cut the throat of any man who shoots at those six. Tell them that, Drum."

Drum grinned wickedly. "Don't worry." Then, silently, he was gone.

Sundance lay there watching the road, Nez Perce all around him in the woods. His Winchester was beside him, but the weapon he intended to use, at least at first, was the taut-strung bow. His quiver was at hand, his arrows laid out neatly. He remembered the slugging boot toe in his ribs, and he thought about what Drury had done to Dead Man Walking; and he had to remind himself that he must somehow take Drury alive and get a signed bill of sale from him. That was hard to think about; what he wanted to do was to kill Luke Drury.

He fitted an arrow to his bow. Then he heard the hoofbeats, as the riders came up the pass.

They approached in single file, the man in the lead bent low, reading sign, and it was Drury. And the horse he rode — Sundance sucked in his breath.

The stallion was huge, its hide white, but splattered from rump to forelock with vari-colored spots, mostly black and roan. Its jaws were bloody, as Drury kept it on a tight rein with a Spanish bit, and there was blood on its flanks, for Drury wore sharp-roweled Spanish spurs. A long quirt dangled from one wrist. He rode Cold Wind Blowing, the best horse the Nez Perce had ever produced, an animal that made even Eagle look awkward by comparison, and he had mastered it with every brutal aid a horseman could use. Even so, Cold Wind Blowing still had fight left in him, great crested neck bowed, quarters gathered, and, as Sundance watched, he lunged against the bit, and Drury ruthlessly tightened rein. The stallion swung and curveted and Drury lashed it to a standstill with the quirt, jerking in hard on the reins. It took all of Sundance's self-control not to loose the arrow in his bow.

The five men behind Luke Drury were cut from the same tough pattern. Hard, bearded professionals from the mining camps, they rode watchfully, eyes sweeping the pines on either side, Winchesters in their hands and ready, most had two guns strapped around their waists. A lot of firepower, Sundance thought, praying that no Nez Perce would let go a premature bullet or arrow. Against superior numbers and superior weapons, all they had on their side was the element of surprise.

But in the pines, everything was absolutely still. Sundance, like all the Indians, lay with head down, not moving a muscle.

Now, at the crest of the pass, Drury

swung off the stallion. Holding its reins tight under its jaw, he bent, examined the road. Sundance had erased all sign of his own presence on it, and after a long moment, Drury straightened up. It was obvious that he was satisfied. He fought the big Appaloosa stallion for a half minute, got his foot in stirrup, then swung back up. He spoke to his men. They wheeled and galloped back down the pass, Drury following. When they had disappeared down the eastern slope, Sundance let out breath. It was all right; soon they would come back and bring the horses.

The wind whispered in the lodgepoles. A few yellowjackets buzzed around Sundance, then flew away. Fifteen minutes passed, and then he smelled them, even before he heard them, caught, on the favorable breeze, the rank odor of sweating horseflesh, mingled with the even ranker one of unwashed white men. Then a mare's whinny and a colt's highpitched braying nicker, and the sound of hoofbeats, and suddenly the horses were there, filing through the pass.

Luke Drury rode in the lead on Cold Wind Blowing, Winchester across his saddle bow. Three more outriders came behind to back him up, their rifles also at the ready. Behind them, a lovely roan-spotted mare led the band, the other mares and foals following and the big stallions in their natural positions on the flanks and in the rear. Hemming them in were seventeen men by Sundance's count, lashing them along with quirts, but all with rifles at the ready.

Everything was as Sundance had hoped it would be, except for the fact that Drury rode Cold Wind Blowing. That presented a problem, for Cold Wind was the most valuable stallion of the herd. Whatever happened, he must not be harmed. Well, Luke Drury was his personal meat, Sundance thought, and he would see to that. He waited, drawing a bow.

Drury's head turned from side to

side, eyes sweeping the pines. His face was unbandaged now, but permanently altered by Sundance's fists, the nose smeared across his craggy countenance, his lips puffed with scar tissue.

The woods seemed to Sundance to vibrate with tension. Every Nez Perce waited for his signal. But he wanted Drury and Cold Wind Blowing across the pass before he gave it.

Then Drury had topped the rise and started down the other side. Sundance lifted the bow and aimed it. The rest of the herd and its outriders were cramped in the pass. He aimed the bow and let the arrow go. A bearded man in a red shirt gasped with astonishment as it passed clean through his chest and out the other side, and then he simply fell off his horse's rump in the path of the oncoming band of Appaloosas.

It was so clean and silent that only the men hard by him even noticed it. One blinked, said: "Hey, what the hell — " They were the last words he ever uttered. Sundance already had another arrow in his bow, and more shafts slotted from the trees, swift and silent and deadly.

Seven men went down under that sheet of arrows. Others yelled, reined in, and suddenly the mountains howled with sound. Sundance threw back his head, shrieked a Cheyenne war whoop, and now he was on his feet, the bow laid aside, the Winchester in his hand, and the Nez Perce were plunging down both hills, firing guns or arrows as they came. Before Drury's men knew what was happening, the Indians leaped from the hillsides, and then each man swung up on a barebacked Appaloosa.

Sundance left the slope in a mighty leap, with all the power of his hardened legs behind it, soared out and down, and landed on the back of a Nez Perce stallion that snorted with surprise. He gripped its mane with one hand, held on as it reared and plunged. As it came down, he heard a man shout: "Injuns!" Another screamed, "Hey, Luke!" That cry ended in a moan of pain. Then a rider loomed up beside Sundance, face contorted, drawn Colt leveled. Sundance passed the Winchester across his body one-handed, pulled the trigger. The heavy slug caught the man and knocked him from the saddle.

The pass was full of mounted Indians, now, and they swung the stallions and mares they rode bareback and attacked the outriders. Sundance saw a sorrel horse go down under the assault of a spotted stallion, heard its rider's despairing cry. It was drowned in Nez Perce war whoops and the roar of guns, as the Indians loosed all their pent-up rage and frustration and hatred. Sundance glimpsed more than one red man fall, but under that assault Drury's men never had a chance.

Sundance knew the stallion under him: Moon Rising, and it had been trained by Yellow Wolf himself. Steady in warfare, superbly responsive to signals and knee pressure, it lanced forward through the turmoil as he touched it with his heels.

He was seeking Drury, whom he'd let go on lest he be killed by mistake. Down the pass, as Sundance broke clear of the melee, he found him. Drury had reined around, was staring, face working. When he saw Sundance thundering toward him, his eyes lit with recognition. "*You!*" he bellowed. He raised his rifle, fired.

Before he pulled the trigger, Sundance dropped, falling beneath the stallion's neck, hanging by a heel across the withers, one hand gripping the mane. The slug cracked through the air where his head had been. Then, gaping at the disappearance of his target, Drury gave way to panic. He jerked Cold Wind around with brutal force, jammed in his spurs. Cold Wind screamed and sprang forward like an arrow from a bow. Sundance came back astride, kicked Moon Rising hard.

Then it was a race. The hooves of the two spotted stallions drummed on the road. Behind, the sound of combat faded. Drury crouched low in the saddle flogging the big Appaloosa, raking it with spurs. Sundance dared not shoot for fear of hitting the horse. Moon Rising ran superbly, but Cold Wind drew slowly away. He was, after all, the greatest stallion the Nez Perce had ever bred.

Sundance's heart sank as the gap widened. Now Drury led him by two hundred yards, increased that by a length and by another. It was murder on both horses, that almost straight downhill race over rutted terrain, and only master horsemen could have kept them on their feet. Sundance was that — but so was Drury.

A mile, two miles, three, it went on and neither horse faltered. The pass was far behind, now, the road twisting and turning like a snake. Once, behind a bend, Drury risked a shot as Sundance charged into sight, but it went wild. Then, confident of escape, Drury wasted no more time.

On either side, thick growths of lodgepoles hemmed them in. The road

232

was hardly more than a gully, dropping straight down. Four miles, now, and nearing five, and a straight stretch ahead, and then Sundance saw it, saw the washout, where water sluicing down the mountain had cut a deep gap a full five feet wide. But that would be no barrier to either horse, an easy jump for both.

Should have been. But as Cold Wind approached it at a dead run, Drury reacted instinctively, tried to pick him up on the bit. The high, sharp port of the cruel spade bit tore at the already lacerated mouth of the stallion that, until a few days before, had never felt anything harsher than a jaw bridle made of rope.

Instead of jumping, Cold Wind screamed and reared and pawed. Taken by surprise, Drury almost fell backwards. Instead, he regained his balance, and instead of falling quit the saddle in a graceful leap, landing like a cat. He made a grab for the stallion's reins, but Cold Wind laid back his ears and his massive jaws nearly chopped off Drury's hand. Drury jerked it back just in time, and then he turned and ran, with Cold Wind right behind him. He made a rock outcropping, scrambled up, and the stallion's charge missed him. Sundance lined his gun, but Drury rolled backwards, disappearing into the woods. The stallion whirled away, pawing at the dragging reins. Sundance caught a glimpse of Drury running through the lodgepoles.

He quit his own stallion in a leap, knowing Moon Rising would stand. Crouched low, he ran up the hill, and Drury snapped a shot at him, but Sundance was already plunging into the trees, and the bullet chugged into a trunk. There was another flash of motion, as Drury retreated farther. Sundance went after him, inexorably, still holding fire.

Drury's big spurs jingled as he ran, it was not hard for Sundance to trail that sound. Crouched low, he whipped around the tree trunks, himself an impossible target in the dimness.

He was used to running, as accustomed to it as riding. He wore moccasins. Drury was a horseman, unseasoned at this kind of footwork in the mountains, and his feet were shod in high-heeled boots. It was no race, no race at all. Once more Drury turned to fire, and Sundance marked the location by the powdersmoke and without answering the fire went out swiftly to the left, knowing that Drury would work back down the slope, make another break for the horses. Sundance made absolutely no sound on the thick pine duff, and he heard the jingling spurs on the slope above and when he was in position took cover behind a fallen tree. He crouched there, motionless, waiting, rifle ready; and then he saw Drury coming down the slope. The big man had thrown away his empty rifle, pulled both sixguns, and the sound of his panting was almost like a locomotive making steam. His head swung from side to side, his eyes wild, his mouth open, gasping. Sundance let him go by, so close to the log he could have hit Drury with the rifle barrel. Then he stood up.

"Drury," he said, voice ringing through the woods. "Drop those guns or you're dead."

Luke Drury froze. "Sundance," he husked, in the voice of a man facing down.

"Drop 'em," Sundance said harshly. For a moment, as Drury stood tensely, it could have gone either way. Then, slowly Drury opened his hands. The two guns fell to earth.

"Turn around."

Drury obeyed. Terror was written across his craggy, broken face. His mouth worked soundlessly. Finally, staring at Sundance's rifle muzzle, he whispered, "What are you? Some kind of goddam ghost — ?" He sucked in his belly, waiting for the inevitable. "Sundance, please . . ."

Sundance only grinned, a grin like the snarl of a hungry wolf. He shoved the rifle forward. "Drury . . . how would you like to stay alive?"

"I'm gonna make a deal with you," Sundance said. "Did the Army give you a formal title to those Nez Perce horses?"

Drury licked his lips. "They gimme a paper, yeah."

"Then you're gonna sign it over to me. In a way that will be completely legal. I want title to those horses. After that, if you're man enough to walk out of these mountains on foot, you can make a try at it." Sundance knew that by then he could have the horses safely in Utah, under the protection of the Mormons, and, as well, signed over to Doris Bucknell. With the full weight of the British government behind her, the Army would not challenge her title.

Drury tried to comprehend this. "You mean — "

"I mean I'm trading you your life for legal title to the horses. And if you try to repudiate it, I'll come after you

237

and hell itself won't be big enough to hide you. You'll never know when or where I'll take you. And when I do, you'll die slow and hard. Don't forget, I'm half Indian and I know all the tricks."

Drury's knees almost buckled. "My life . . . for God's sake, yes, Sundance. You can have it, you can have those God damned horses."

"Where's the title?"

"In my saddle bags down yonder on the stallion."

"All right," Sundance said. "We're going down slow and easy. If you break, you're dead."

Drury was too smart to break. With lifted hands, he marched down the slope, Sundance right behind. Out on the road, the two stallions waited, Moon Rising calm, Cold Wind still nervous, blood dripping from jaws and flanks. Sundance had Drury stand fast, keeping the gun on him, as he went to the stallion, spoke softly to it, touched it soothingly, then unfastened the saddle bags. It flinched, but otherwise stood fast.

Sundance tossed the saddle bags to Drury. "You got pen and ink in there?"

Drury nodded. His hands shook as he fumbled with the bags. Sundance watched him carefully. Drury took out a folded paper. "Read it to me," Sundance said, and Drury did in a shaky voice. It was long and legalistic, and it was signed by the adjutant of the Regiment that had found the horses, and it gave Drury absolute ownership of the spotted stallions and their mares. "All right," Sundance said. "Get ready to write."

Drury took out pen, an ink bottle, opened it, laid the paper on the bags, and Sundance dictated. When he was through, he said, "Sign it." The pen scratched as Drury obeyed. Still keeping the rifle on him, Sundance said, "Bring it here." Drury came to him with the saddlebags over his arm, the paper in his hand. It shook as he held it out to Sundance.

Drury's scrawl was hardly readable, but it was in order, Sundance saw, letting his eyes flick over it, but still keeping tight watch of Drury.

"All right," he said. He held the paper out to dry in one hand and lowered the rifle. "You can turn around now and start walking."

"Sundance, for God's sake, I'll need blankets, grub."

"That's your worry," Sundance said. "You're alive. Be glad of that. Maybe you can find your guns up in the woods. If you're as smart as an Indian, Drury, you'll be all right. Now, on your way."

Drury's face worked, but he turned, the saddlebags still across his arm, and began to walk. Sundance watched him teeter down the slope for twenty yards in his high-heeled boots, and then he let out a long breath and turned toward Moon Rising.

At that instant, the other stallion,

Cold Wind, snorted. Something in the sound made Sundance whirl. Down the slope, Drury had turned, was on his knees. He held in his right hand the short-barreled Colt he'd taken from the saddle bags, steadied his aim with his left. His face was contorted with rage and hatred. "Goddam you!" he yelled, and Sundance raised the rifle.

He was too late. Drury pulled the trigger.

But he was too late. At the sound of Drury's voice, Cold Wind Blowing had already pinned back his ears and charged straight down the hill for Drury. The sight of twelve hundred pounds of maddened Appaloosa made Drury jerk, threw off his aim.

Then he swung the gun barrel toward the stallion, but he was too late.

There was nothing Sundance could do. Drury's treatment of the big horse had set a flame of hatred burning in the Appaloosa's brain. It had flickered low, but not gone out, and that wild shout had made it flare. Drury jumped to his feet, tried to run, but then the stallion had him.

Its great head stretched out, its huge jaws seized his arm. Drury screamed as Cold Wind reared, shaking him like a terrier with a rat. He kicked as he dangled from the horse's mouth, and his scream died, as a huge, hard forefoot caught him in the ribs. Then Cold Wind let him drop. Drury fell limply and Cold Wind pawed at him, and Sundance heard something crunch. Then the stallion turned and kicked at the thing on the ground and whirled again and savaged it with his jaws some more, and Sundance stood clear. Cold Wind would kill him just as quickly if he went to the big horse in its rage. Instead, Sundance swung up on the other stallion.

There was nothing he could do but wait. Cold Wind Blowing's rage lasted perhaps five minutes. Then he was satisfied with what he had done. He snorted, and red drops flew from his jaws as he shook his head, turned and trotted back up the pass.

Sundance let him go, knowing he was headed back toward where he had last seen his mares. Cold Wind went swiftly, and Sundance followed on the other stallion.

## 10

DORIS was pale-faced and shaking with reaction. "Jim," she whispered. "Oh, it was terrible . . . "

Sundance already knew that. He had seen what the Nez Perce had done to Drury's men, of whom, they claimed, none had escaped. All he could say as he held her tightly was, "They had a lot of long over-due debts to pay."

He looked at the band of spotted horses grazing on the floor of this small, well-hidden canyon in the Bitterroots, to which they had been brought immediately. With them were most of the mounts of Drury's men, carefully rounded up by the Nez Perce after the battle. It had been important to leave no trace of what had happened. Drury and all his gunmen were buried under tons of rock beneath a cliff where shale and talus had made it easy to start a slide. Carefully, the Indians had cleaned up the battle site. It would be to any investigators as if they had started over the mountains and then had simply vanished from the face of the earth.

Now he and Doris were here beside a smokeless fire with most of the Nez Perce ranged around them, and it was the first chance he and she and Yellow Wolf had had to talk. Sundance released her and fished in the pocket of his pants, bringing out a bill-fold from which he took a document.

"It's been rough," he told her, "but anyhow, it's all in order now. Here's a legal bill of sale to me from Drury for the horses. I'll sign it over to you, and after everybody's rested, we'll strike out for Utah."

"Yes," she said. "Please. Sign it over to me right away."

There was so much urgency in her voice that Jim Sundance looked at her curiously. But he had Drury's pen and ink, and he laid the document on a flat stone and began to write. Presently, he straightened up. "Here it is. Maybe it wouldn't stand up for an American, but your government will make sure it's honored."

"Yes," she said. "The Queen will see to that. Let me have that pen, please. And is there any more paper?"

Sundance stared.

"I want to write a draft for the other twenty thousand dollars," she said. "You've fulfilled your bargain."

Sundance gave her paper from Drury's saddle bags. She wrote carefully and passed it to him. "It will take a few weeks for it to clear New York," she said, "but the money's on deposit there. Thank you, Jim."

Sundance said quietly, "The thanks are due to you. Even if this doesn't buy Joseph's way back home, it'll buy the Nez Perce better land than they've got now. At least they'll survive." He started to reach for the pen, but she drew it away.

"One moment," she said. "I'm not through yet." She unfolded the bill of sale, and in the last clear space on it, began to write. When she was finished she waved it to dry it, and then she handed it to Yellow Wolf, who looked at it blankly.

"Tell him, Jim," she said, "that the Queen will honor it. When he gets the horses back to Canada, no one will take them from him."

Sundance frowned. "Canada?"

Doris smiled. "Remember? The night before the battle, I talked with Yellow Wolf alone. I told him then that I couldn't do it." Her voice faltered. "I simply couldn't, Jim. These aren't my horses and they never could be. They could never be anybody's horses but the Nez Perce's."

"I don't understand," Sundance said. He looked at the draft.

"Yellow Wolf did. He wanted those horses desperately, but he told me that Joseph wouldn't allow it. A bargain had been made, and Joseph would insist that it be kept. So would he, because he had given his word. So . . . " She shrugged. "The bargain's kept. You've delivered the horses and title for them to me, and I've chosen to give them to the Nez Perce." Her voice deepened. "They don't belong in England, Jim, and they don't belong in India. They belong here, in the mountains, with the men who bred them. They are . . . my memorial to John. He died here for them, and this is where I want him honored and remembered. This way he'll have more dignity in death than if I had taken them home to be curiosities, just the fruit of a rich man's whim. John deserved better than that. So do the Nez Perces and so do the spotted horses."

Sundance looked at her and at the grinning Yellow Wolf, and translated to make sure Yellow Wolf understood, and then he groped for words. All he could find to say was, "I had already judged you as a thoroughbred. I was right."

She smiled. "In the circles in which I move, that is a high compliment indeed."

Sundance looked at Yellow Wolf. "You can get the horses to Canada?"

"I'll get them there," Yellow Wolf said. "Jim, you come too and bring her with you. She is much woman."

Doris understood that, and she shook her head. "No. No, we have to go on to Utah." She paused. "I wish I could stay here. Oh, how I wish it. I would like to go to Canada with the Nez Perce and live there and . . . But I told you, Jim. I must go home. I want you, if you will, to take me to Utah where I can take a train."

"Brigham City," Sundance said.

"Yes." Doris paused and her eyes met Sundance's. "But . . . I hope it's not too short a trip."

Slowly Sundance grinned.

"We can drag it out," he said.

Doris smiled. "Good. I am in no hurry at all. Absolutely none."

Yellow Wolf had put the paper in

his medicine bag, a sacred place where it would be absolutely safe; he wore it around his neck on a bearclaw chain. Now, he said. "Wait a minute."

Sundance and Doris looked at him as he swung up on his horse. "What — ?" she asked.

But Jim Sundance already understood. "You just gave him a present, the greatest one possible. He has to give you something in return."

They watched as Yellow Wolf rode into the horse herd. When he returned, the stallion Moon Rising, a fine, broadhipped breeding mare, and a filly followed him like trained dogs.

Yellow Wolf drew himself up and gestured toward the three horses. "These three," he said, "the woman must take to Utah and then across the water. If anyone has questions, you can say they came from Lapwai. It is something you can manage, Sundance."

"Sure," Sundance said. "I can manage it."

250

Doris' face lit with delight. "May I?"

"You have to," Sundance said. "Every time you look at them in England, remember the Nez Perce. Just as, every time one of them sees a spotted stallion, he'll think of Lady Bucknell."

"Jim," she whispered, and she went to Moon Rising and stroked his head. He took it gently, nickering softly.

"Neither the mare nor the filly is Moon Rising's get," Yellow Wolf said. "Later, if she wants fresh blood for the line, she can bring it from Lapwai." Then he whirled his mount and rode back toward the herd.

Doris watched him go. The sun was going down behind the mountains. In its last rays, the spotted vari-colored horses grazing on the canyon floor were as vivid as so many jewels. A mare raised her head and nickered, an Appaloosa stallion whinnied, pawed the earth and neighed.

The sound echoed from hill to hill

as Sundance and Doris turned away
and went up the canyon to where their
robes were spread.

# THE END

*Other titles in the*
*Linford Western Library:*

## TOP HAND
### Wade Everett

The Broken T was big. But no ranch is big enough to let a man hide from himself.

## GUN WOLVES OF LOBO BASIN
### Lee Floren

The Feud was a blood debt. When Smoke Talbot found the outlaws who gunned down his folks he aimed to nail their hide to the barn door.

## SHOTGUN SHARKEY
### Marshall Grover

The westbound coach carrying the indomitable Larry and Stretch headed for a shooting showdown.

## FIGHTING RAMROD
### Charles N. Heckelmann

Most men would have cut their
losses, but Frazer counted the bullets
in his guns and said he'd soak the
range in blood before he'd give up
another inch of what was his.


## LONE GUN
### Eric Allen

Smoke Blackbird had been away too
long. The Lequires had seized the
Blackbird farm, forcing the Indians
and settlers off, and no one seemed
willing to fight! He had to fight
alone.


## THE THIRD RIDER
### Barry Cord

Mel Rawlins wasn't going to let
anything stand in his way. His father
was murdered, his two brothers
gone. Now Mel rode for vengeance.

## ARIZONA DRIFTERS
### W. C. Tuttle

When drifting Dutton and Lonnie Steelman decide to become partners they find that they have a common enemy in the formidable Thurston brothers.

## TOMBSTONE
### Matt Braun

Wells Fargo paid Luke Starbuck to outgun the silver-thieving stagecoach gang at Tombstone. Before long Luke can see the only thing bearing fruit in this eldorado will be the gallows tree.

## HIGH BORDER RIDERS
### Lee Floren

Buckshot McKee and Tortilla Joe cut the trail of a border tough who was running Mexican beef into Texas. They stopped the smuggler in his tracks.

## BRETT RANDALL, GAMBLER
### E. B. Mann

Larry Day had the choice of running away from the law or of assuming a dead man's place. No matter what he decided he was bound to end up dead.

## THE GUNSHARP
### William R. Cox

The Eggerleys weren't very smart. They trained their sights on Will Carney and Arizona's biggest blood bath began.

## THE DEPUTY OF SAN RIANO
### Lawrence A. Keating and
### Al. P. Nelson

When a man fell dead from his horse, Ed Grant was spotted riding away from the scene. The deputy sheriff rode out after him and came up against everything from gunfire to dynamite.

## FARGO: MASSACRE RIVER
### John Benteen

The ambushers up ahead had now blocked the road. Fargo's convoy was a jumble, a perfect target for the insurgents' weapons!

## SUNDANCE: DEATH IN THE LAVA
### John Benteen

The Modoc's captured the wagon train and its cargo of gold. But now the halfbreed they called Sundance was going after it . . .

## HARSH RECKONING
### Phil Ketchum

Five years of keeping himself alive in a brutal prison had made Brand tough and careless about who he gunned down . . .

# FARGO: PANAMA GOLD
## John Benteen

With foreign money behind him, Buckner was going to destroy the Panama Canal before it could be completed. Fargo's job was to stop Buckner.

# FARGO:
# THE SHARPSHOOTERS
## John Benteen

The Canfield clan, thirty strong were raising hell in Texas. Fargo was tough enough to hold his own against the whole clan.

# PISTOL LAW
## Paul Evan Lehman

Lance Jones came back to Mustang for just one thing — revenge! Revenge on the people who had him thrown in jail.

## HELL RIDERS
### Steve Mensing

Wade Walker's kid brother, Duane, was locked up in the Silver City jail facing a rope at dawn. Wade was a ruthless outlaw, but he was smart, and he had vowed to have his brother out of jail before morning!

## DESERT OF THE DAMNED
### Nelson Nye

The law was after him for the murder of a marshal — a murder he didn't commit. Breen was after him for revenge — and Breen wouldn't stop at anything . . . blackmail, a frameup . . . or murder.

## DAY OF THE COMANCHEROS
### Steven C. Lawrence

Their very name struck terror into men's hearts — the Comancheros, a savage army of cutthroats who swept across Texas, leaving behind a bloodstained trail of robbery and murder.

# SUNDANCE: SILENT ENEMY
## John Benteen

A lone crazed Cheyenne was on a personal war path. They needed to pit one man against one crazed Indian. That man was Sundance.

# LASSITER
## Jack Slade

Lassiter wasn't the kind of man to listen to reason. Cross him once and he'll hold a grudge for years to come — if he let you live that long.

# LAST STAGE TO GOMORRAH
## Barry Cord

Jeff Carter, tough ex-riverboat gambler, now had himself a horse ranch that kept him free from gunfights and card games. Until Sturvesant of Wells Fargo showed up.

# McALLISTER ON THE COMANCHE CROSSING
## Matt Chisholm

The Comanche, McAllister owes them a life — and the trail is soaked with the blood of the men who had tried to outrun them before.

# QUICK-TRIGGER COUNTRY
## Clem Colt

Turkey Red hooked up with Curly Bill Graham's outlaw crew. But wholesale murder was out of Turk's line, so when range war flared he bucked the whole border gang alone . . .

# CAMPAIGNING
## Jim Miller

Ambushed on the Santa Fe trail, Sean Callahan is saved by two Indian strangers. But there'll be more lead and arrows flying before the band join Kit Carson against the Comanches.

## GUNSLINGER'S RANGE
### Jackson Cole

Three escaped convicts are out for revenge. They won't rest until they put a bullet through the head of the dirty snake who locked them behind bars.

## RUSTLER'S TRAIL
### Lee Floren

Jim Carlin knew he would have to stand up and fight because he had staked his claim right in the middle of Big Ike Outland's best grass.

## THE TRUTH ABOUT SNAKE RIDGE
### Marshall Grover

The troubleshooters came to San Cristobal to help the needy. For Larry and Stretch the turmoil began with a brawl and then an ambush.

## WOLF DOG RANGE
### Lee Floren

Will Ardery would stop at nothing, unless something stopped him first — like a bullet from Pete Manly's gun.

## DEVIL'S DINERO
### Marshall Grover

Plagued by remorse, a rich old reprobate hired the Texas Trouble-shooters to deliver a fortune in greenbacks to each of his victims.

## GUNS OF FURY
### Ernest Haycox

Dane Starr, alias Dan Smith, wanted to close the door on his past and hang up his guns, but people wouldn't let him.

## DONOVAN
### Elmer Kelton

Donovan was supposed to be dead. Uncle Joe Vickers had fired off both barrels of a shotgun into the vicious outlaw's face as he was escaping from jail. Now Uncle Joe had been shot — in just the same way.

## CODE OF THE GUN
### Gordon D. Shirreffs

MacLean came riding home, with saddle tramp written all over him, but sewn in his shirt-lining was an Arizona Ranger's star.

## GAMBLER'S GUN LUCK
### Brett Austen

Gamblers seldom live long. Parker was a hell of a gambler. It was his life — or his death . . .

## ORPHAN'S PREFERRED
### Jim Miller

Sean Callahan answers the call of the Pony Express and fights Indians and outlaws to get the mail through.


## DAY OF THE BUZZARD
### T. V. Olsen

All Val Penmark cared about was getting the men who killed his wife.


## THE MANHUNTER
### Gordon D. Shirreffs

Lee Kershaw knew that every Rurale in the territory was on the lookout for him. But the offer of $5,000 in gold to find five small pieces of leather was too good to turn down.

# RIFLES ON THE RANGE
## Lee Floren

Doc Mike and the farmer stood there alone between Smith and Watson. There was this moment of stillness, and then the roar would start. And somebody would die . . .

# HARTIGAN
## Marshall Grover

Hartigan had come to Cornerstone to die. He chose the time and the place, and Main Street became a battlefield.

# SUNDANCE: OVERKILL
## John Benteen

When a wealthy banker's daughter was kidnapped by the Cheyenne, he offered Sundance $10,000 to rescue the girl.